LES BELLE

Louise Lévêque de Vilmorin (1902–1969) was a French novelist, poet and journalist. She is best known for her novel *Madame De...* filmed as *The Earrings of Madame De...* in 1953. Her romantic life included an engagement to Antoine de Saint-Exupéry.

John Preston is a former Arts Editor of the *Evening Standard* and the *Sunday Telegraph*. He was the *Sunday Telegraph*'s Television Critic for sixteen years. He is the author of four novels, including *The Dig*.

Les Belles Amours

Les Belles Amours

_____

Louise de Vilmorin

Translated by Francis Wyndham

FOREWORD BY JOHN PRESTON

With drawings by Dodie Masterman

CAPUCHIN CLASSICS

CAPUCHIN CLASSICS
LONDON

Les Belles Amours

French Edition © Editions Gallimard, Paris 1954

English language translation © Francis Wyndham 1956

Foreword © John Preston 2012

This edition published by Capuchin Classics 2012

Thanks to Fairless Masterman for his kind permission
to reproduce the drawings of Dodie Masterman

2 4 6 8 0 9 7 5 3 1

Capuchin Classics
128 Kensington Church Street, London W8 4BH
Telephone: +44 (0)20 7221 7166
Fax: +44 (0)20 7792 9288
E-mail: info@capuchin-classics.co.uk
www.capuchin-classics.co.uk

Châtelaine of Capuchin Classics: Emma Howard

Cover design by Stephanie Clair

ISBN: 978-1-907429-54-5

Printed and bound by CPI Group (UK) Ltd, Croydon CR0 4YY.

To
Orson Welles

Contents

Foreword

Les Belles Amours is a novel about romantic liaisons, and no one could accuse its author of not knowing what she was writing about. Louise Lévêque de Vilmorin's own love life was an extremely tangled, many-branched affair which included an affair with Orson Welles – to whom Les Belles Amours is dedicated – an engagement to Antoine de Saint-Exupéry – who briefly gave up flying for her sake – and long involvements with both the French writer André Malraux and Duff Cooper, the then British ambassador in Paris. She was also believed to have been unusually close to Duff Cooper's wife, Lady Diana.

If on the face of it de Vilmorin seemed an unlikely femme fatale – she walked with a pronounced limp – she plainly had a magnetic allure. Francis Wyndham, who translated Les Belles Amours, remembers going to see her in Paris with his friend, Colin Tennant. Invited to her house, they were surprised to find it apparently deserted. Just as they were about to leave, an upstairs window was flung open and there was de Vilmorin – then in her sixties – wearing French national costume and with her hair in pigtails. 'You couldn't say she was beautiful, but there was an aura about her. In some mysterious way, she was tremendously attractive.'

For such an avowed bohemian, she had a solidly haut bourgeois upbringing. The heir to a great fortune – Vilmorin is still the biggest seed company in France – she was brought up in the family château outside Paris. Soon after her engagement to Saint Exupéry fell through, she married an American real-estate heir, Henry Leigh Hunt, whose father owned most of Las Vegas.

When this marriage failed, another soon followed – to a Hungarian playboy whose second wife (de Vilmorin was his fifth) had owned two Derby winners. This too came unstuck, but de Vilmorin, never one to repine for long, then became the mistress of the husband of one of her former husband's wives – I did warn you this was a complicated story.

Along the way she began to write – carefully observed, delicately wrought stories usually set against an aristocratic or artistic background. De Vilmorin's best-known novel, *Madame De...* was filmed as *The Earrings of Madame De...* by Max Ophüls. Once called 'the most perfect film ever made' by the American critic Andrew Sarris, it follows the fortunes of a pair of earrings as they pass from hand to hand.

Les Belles Amours, written in the mid fifties, is in similar vein. The main character – Monsieur Zaraguirre – is a middle-aged man, enormously successful with women, who nonetheless manages to stay emotionally insulated from his lovers. 'To love him was to regret him,' de Vilmorin writes. 'His kiss did not diminish his essential remoteness.'

But passing agreeably through his fifties, Zarraguirre falls helplessly in love with the fiancée of his son's best friend – a woman many epochs his junior. De Vilmorin is particularly good at what one might term the physical mechanics of falling in love. To his alarm, Zaraguirre finds that 'his heart had changed its rhythm: he had the sensation of slowness, weight and silence.'

But however violently de Vilmorin's characters may fall in love, there's always a sliver of distrust somewhere in the backs of their minds – a suspicion that feelings which have tumbled so precipitously in one direction could easily tumble in another. Fidelity here is presented not so much as a hopeless aspiration as a biological impossibility. What's more, to engage in lasting fidelity – even if it were possible – would be to cut oneself off from what de Vilmorin clearly considers to be one of the great pleasures of love – guilt.

When Zaraguirre's now-wife meets up with her former fiancée and finds her heart beating a little faster than anticipated, she 'did not reason and try to control herself, but gave herself up to it, took the side of her guilt and delighted in it.'

All this, of course, makes it a very French novel. Indeed, I would say that you will seldom, if ever, read a book that confirms quite so many stereotypes about the French as *Les Belles Amours*. As well as being extremely randy, everyone in it is also prone to making windy pronouncements about life. 'Caution is fruitless and the spirit of reason is of small account beside instinct,' declares Zaraguirre at one point – and even at his moment of deepest crisis, the aphorisms still keep coming thick and fast.

Priapic one moment, philosophical the next . . . It could easily have proved a numbing combination. But de Vilmorin traces her characters' emotional buffetings with great acuity, wryness and affection. Although she never condemns them for the way their affections slew about, neither does she let them off the moral hook. The result is a novel whose elements, when broken down into individual chunks, may not look that promising – but which, when put together, possess an unusual charm and allure. Much like de Vilmorin herself, in fact.

John Preston

Part One

Whenever there was a question of love, M. Zaraguirre said that to love is to invent and he also said that love fills the imagination before taking possession of the heart. He was a brave and wilful man, without vanity or arrogance. His childhood had been lulled more by sighs than by songs, and he remembered it as an isle of sadness from which he had escaped early to conquer other realities. He had experienced adventure, work and success. The spirit of observation, even livelier in him than emotion, had made his fortune and continued to secure it, but this fortune, which he saw as the fruit of good sense and the result of orderly feeling, was often attributed to luck, that is to say to the lack of moral equilibrium in human destiny.

M. Zaraguirre lived in South America where he had founded large companies; he had simple tastes and refused to belong to any society. From the gentle fire which could be felt to burn beneath his cold appearance there rose an occasional flame which made him seem sensual and inconstant, but in reality he believed in love, in other favours and other fervours than those of pleasure.

His manner, his fortune, his reputation for intelligence and the attention paid him by everyone made an impression on women; watching him, they tried to meet his look and if they were at all agreeable he gave them a smile which put them at his mercy. He rather liked them. The disadvantages that a man of his sort, occupied and preoccupied by the expression of very different inclinations, ideas and gifts, finds in being loved too passionately, always made him tend to be cautious, and if he did not resist certain temptations, if he knew how to be affectionate and patient, he fled from reproaches and refused to make promises. His choice caused in its object an intoxication made of hope and pride, and she immediately found herself surrounded by mirages which tears of doubt slowly dispersed. To love him was to regret him, his kiss did not diminish his essential remoteness, liberty could be divined beneath his ardour and independence showed through his fidelity. He inspired and disarmed possessiveness, and as he was inaccessible women longed to own him. 'Ask me for anything you want, except a promise,' he told them, and when, tired of uncertainty, wishing also to hold a pledge of their reign, they came to prefer jewels to kisses, he agreed with them and, considering that so much wisdom deserved a reward, sent them a diamond ring. This was his parting gift, which was accompanied by a few simple words: 'The solitaire is my emblem, a sad one,' he wrote, 'do not make it yours. Accept it, forget it, it is a goodbye kiss.'

Although men criticised on principle this easy method of choosing and discarding women, they secretly admired it, while the women hid in their hearts a nostalgia for their lost love and, smiling, making the best of a bad bargain, compared M. Zaraguirre to an impregnable fortress. But they were wrong. M. Zaraguirre had reached his fifty-sixth year when, during a journey in France, he fell desperately in love with the fiancée of Louis Duville who happened to be the son of his greatest friends. Nothing more deplorable could have happened.

MM. Duville father and son were seed merchants. Together they ran a commercial firm long established in the provinces; they understood each other perfectly in the management of their business, and managed it as they did their private lives, with serious good humour and kind authority. They were alike in this but not in other ways. Whereas the father had found happiness in the shadow of duty and in respect for tradition, M. Louis Duville, his son, derived his pleasure from less severe sources, and passed his hours of leisure each week in Paris, with pretty women and friends as rich and extravagant as himself. He had a flat on the left bank of the Seine. Louis Duville was not bohemian but he was said to be a libertine, and he had had numerous mistresses, all dangerous in the eyes of his parents who were worried by this state of affairs. They feared to see him marry a girl from heaven knew where, or that a fatal love for a married woman would prevent him from founding a home similar to the one of which he was the centre. Nevertheless, by not exhorting him to follow their example, by showing him

neither anger nor sorrow, they had kept his confidence and the three of them formed a happy family.

Valronce, their country house, had been built under the Consulate. It was situated in the near neighbourhood of the town to which they were called by business every day, and its park, famous for its collection of rare plants, surrounded it with a vast shade and placed it in the heart of an exotic region.

M. Duville and M. Zaraguirre were old friends. They hid nothing from each other, they relied on each other and amused themselves when together with obscure jokes which evoked, for them alone, incidents and faces from their youth. At Valronce, M. Zaraguirre relaxed the impression he made everywhere else of being a foreigner; he gave himself up there to the delights of affection and laughed with the beautiful young girls whom Mme Duville never stopped inviting in the hope that her son would fall in love with one of them. Louis Duville fell in love with none; he did not seem to be destined to become a husband, and, indifferent to his mother's disappointment, he let them get married one after the other. Mme Duville was very persistent: she went to the weddings, inspected the bridesmaids, and bid the prettiest come to Valronce to fill the place left empty by the latest bride. These young girls showed M. Zaraguirre a glimpse of the happy youth which fate had denied him, and also gave him the impression of being at the same time their brother, father and grandfather. In the evening, when Mme Duville took her place at the piano, he danced with them; M. Duville and his son did the same, and the three men allowed themselves to be led in round dances through the house and in the garden. October brought to Valronce the gayest moments of the year. M. Zaraguirre felt at home under this domestic roof; he was happy there but he knew that his life lay elsewhere, and, at the end of two weeks, as though afraid of weakening, he left again for distant lands where, still remaining himself, he obeyed the demands of a character in whom the Duvilles would not have recognised their friend.

If Louis Duville liked speed, late nights, casual love affairs and race-meetings, he shared with his father a love of nature and a pride in the family business. Pleasure did not make him neglect his work. A success with women, he was easily bored and he was thirty years old when he became engaged to be married.

Carried away by love, he made up his mind from one moment to the next, without thinking it over, so certain was he of his love. It is true that the violence of love makes patience impossible; however, it was not only love, it was doubtless a presentiment which made him wish to be married at once, without waiting.

* * *

Fate often reveals itself in mysterious ways which appear to be chance. Mme Duville was very fond of one of her cousins; he was a colonel and she was understandably proud of this fact. On the 18th of September, 1925, while she was shopping in the town, she met him by chance at the pastry-cook's, just before midday. He told her that he had recently retired, which he minded, and perhaps to comfort himself he was eating a cream cake.

'Retired! At last! What good news!' said Mme Duville. 'We shall see more of you. Come to lunch at Valronce on Saturday.

Have you reopened your house? I hope so, it certainly needed it. Well, can you come on Saturday?'

'Saturday, no, on Saturday I'm expecting my nephew's wife . . .'

'Your nephew? I thought he died in 1918.'

'Heroism doesn't kill everybody,' replied the colonel. 'My nephew is dead, but his wife is alive; she's only twenty-five and I try to distract her. The war, you know,' he went on, 'it's always the same story; no war no history, and without war where would we be and what would happen to history? Ah! if only they'd listened to me . . .'

Mme Duville interrupted him: 'Nobody listens to anybody, I hate wars, and don't show off, I can't stand that. Bring your niece to lunch, we shall be pleased to see her. Louis won't be there, he always goes out on Saturdays. Where? You'll never guess: to Paris! When he was twenty I could understand it, but what does he go there for now he's thirty?'

The colonel went: 'Hmm . . . Hmm . . .' and said no more.

On her return to Valronce, Mme Duville told her husband that she had met the colonel and that he had accepted her invitation to bring his niece to lunch in two days' time. 'He has retired, he has reopened Dentelle. That will give us a new neighbour, I'm glad, aren't you?' M. Duville nodded. Kindness often prevented him from replying.

Two days later, Louis Duville was about to leave Valronce when a car drew up behind his own at the front door. The colonel got nimbly out of it, then gave his hand to a young woman who immediately came into view. Louis Duville greeted his cousin, was introduced to the lady and showed them to the library. They had arrived early, and as neither M. nor Mme Duville were there politeness obliged him to keep them company. The young woman admired the pictures; she said, 'Ah!' several times and this exclamation, though simple, attracted Louis Duville's attention. 'Ah! What an interesting man,' she said of a portrait. 'What a face, what a forehead! He is a little like you.' He asked

her if she were a foreigner. 'I know,' she answered, 'I have a Spanish accent.'

'Foreigner,' said the colonel, 'that's a word I don't like. She's not a foreigner, but she was brought up in Spain, where her father was military attaché.'

'Yes, for five years, but I stayed more than ten years in a convent at Madrid. I only came to France in the holidays, and when I was seventeen I suddenly got married.'

'In Spain?' asked Louis Duville.

'No, in France,' replied the colonel, and after praising the character, career and merits of his nephew he began to describe the military exploit in which he had lost his life.

His niece could not hide the distress which this story caused her. Her attitude was one of resignation; her lips parted in an assumed smile, she blushed and Louis Duville chanced to notice it. She turned to him, shrugged her shoulders as if to say 'What can one do?' and they exchanged a glance which made them seem accomplices. They were sitting at opposite ends of a long sofa, and while the colonel rambled on, stopped and started again in search of his breath and the thread of his thought, they smiled at each other behind his back and even winked. This mutual understanding did not last long. At first surprised, then serious, then more and more oblivious of their immediate surroundings, they gradually felt that pleasant uneasiness which always betrays attraction and sometimes foretells love. The disturbance felt by Louis Duville prevented him from moving. His imagination was confused, his heart changed its rhythm, he had the sensation of slowness, weight and silence, and he no longer wanted to leave.

'Courage is a dangerous weapon which has a habit of turning round against one. Handling it is a very delicate business. Of course, one has to arm oneself with courage, but one must know how to get rid of it at the right moment. That's the whole question: no courage, no army, too much courage and there's no army left. As for me . . .' the colonel was saying when Mme Duville came in.

'Bravo!' she cried.

The colonel only replied by introducing his niece, and there followed a friendly conversation which Mme Duville interrupted by asking her son, 'So you haven't gone?'

'I was waiting for you,' he answered. On which he said goodbye and left.

In the hall he met his father who was also surprised by his presence. 'Have you changed your plans?'

'To tell you the truth, I am hesitating. It is late, and I am not feeling well.'

'Then don't drive on the main roads. You know what they're like in September. Tell them to lay a place for you at lunch, and stay here. It's more prudent.'

M. Duville waited for his son and they went arm-in-arm to the library.

During lunch, as they were discussing heroism, M. Duville quoted M. Zaraguirre: '"Whether it be a cathedral, a poem, a work of art or a hero, nothing makes itself felt, nothing survives except by exaggeration" that's what our friend Zaraguirre says.'

Louis Duville did not take part in the conversation.

'You have a sore throat. You're starting a cold,' his mother told him.

'Possibly,' he answered, and that was all. He was waiting for the moment when the young woman sitting opposite him, her face bent over the table, would look at him without lifting her head; and he thought of nothing but that look which made him languid and forgetful. Silently they must have told each other many things, for towards the end of lunch he asked her to walk with him in the deep shade of the trees. She accepted and, making several remarks on the late-blooming flowers and their moist scent, she followed him into the garden.

'I stayed because of you,' he said.

'Because of me?'

'Yes, it was you who kept me here, and in a moment you will know why.'

It had rained in the morning. The water, dripping from the shrubs, had formed little holes in the sand on the edge of the paths, and she remarked on this.

Resemblance contains a blend of positive and negative qualities. Neither dark nor fair, but with medium colouring and features, she was one of those women who, recalling every type of beauty yet offending none, are near relations to great beauties and rightly give pleasure. Louis Duville would have preferred to walk behind her rather than at her side, the better to imagine her. She moved with such light and careless steps that she seemed to be carried along by the breeze, and there was something innocent and detached about her whole personality, something strange yet very simple which teasingly provoked audacity. She continued to smile. Her white felt hat was trimmed with a wreath of ivy. 'They are real leaves. You can touch them,' she said. He lightly stroked them with a finger; they stopped for a moment and she added: 'It was my idea.'

'Have you been happy?' he asked her.

'You ask me that question as though you were jealous. What do you want me to answer? Boredom is a form of sadness that I know quite well. That's all. I live in the East of France, with my brother and his wife, I am not unhappy, and then I have my dogs.'

'Is that all?'

'It is and it isn't. As you can imagine, we have many neighbours who like enjoying themselves. There are picnics, hunting, small dances and, when there is nothing better to do, we play cards. I lead the life of people who live in the country and look after their estates. Only, I am alone, so it is monotonous. You at least have a big business and a large town nearby, and then you have Paris.'

'True,' answered Louis Duville; 'however, I would sooner never see Paris again than do without your beautiful voice in the future.'

Her voice had a gentle cooing sound; her speech seemed to be accompanied by a tenuous roll of drums which rose from the distance, died on her lips and clarified the slightest word she said; it was like a relic of her childhood in a foreign land and it made an experienced man want to approach her, to know her better and to take her away with him to share an unconventional life.

'Ah, Paris,' she said, 'I've never been there.'

After reaching the boundary of the park they crossed a wasteland on which only brambles grew, and found themselves on the edge of a yellowish common where some euphorbia was trembling.

'Let us go back to the park. Ah! these flowers, I wouldn't pick them for anything in the world. I'd be too afraid of catching their sadness. Here I'd be frightened of a hare or a bird. Of course, one can easily be frightened of birds. But what a desert! What a desolate place!'

'We will be even more alone here,' said Louis Duville.

She accompanied him unwillingly to the edge of a road, beside which there was a large pile of stones.

'Come, we will sit here like a king and a queen on a throne of fortune,' he told her, and before she had time to understand he lifted her in his arms, placed her on top of one of the stones, sat down beside her, took her hands, lifted them slowly to his lips and said: 'I never want to leave you, will you live with me?'

'I haven't thought about it.'

'Well, then, think about it. Or rather, don't think about it, dream about it, because dreams go further than thoughts.'

'I will dream about it tonight.'

'No, start dreaming now.'

'I am dreaming,' she said.

'Then go to sleep.'

'I seem to have done nothing else all my life.' She closed her eyes and murmured: 'It is true that dreams go far. I am carried away.'

'Don't go too far.'

'I am travelling towards you but you are still very distant.'

He kissed her, they looked at each other and there was nothing more to say.

Eternity is glimpsed at the start of a love affair. They felt that in an instant they had become a couple who would never again know indifference; the happiness they experienced seemed inaccessible and they rejoiced in the idea of being what they were. He was handsome; she combined great passion with great grace, and an inexpressible pride in loving each other mingled with their love and made it yet more beautiful. The dismal heath appeared to be enchanted; they lingered to pick some euphorbia and decided to make it the emblem of their beautiful love. Their recent memories were already attached to the landscape as they returned, giving their surroundings a quality of intimacy and romantic perfection. When they reached Valronce they found that tea had been served some time ago.

'We called you,' Mme Duville told them, 'but you could not have heard.'

'I even shouted "Oo-oo!"' the colonel specified, 'and I haven't done that for at least twenty years. My dear child,' he said to his niece, 'have you any idea of the time?'

'No.'

'I thought not; but time is important even if you do despise it. Victory and defeat are a question of time. Come, it is getting dark and I don't like driving at night.'

'We let ourselves get carried away,' said Louis Duville.

'I can understand that. Going for a walk is a form of exploration and it is such an agreeable kind that one does get carried away,' said M. Duville.

'One wants to go on till one has discovered the surprises on the horizon: just one more tree, another splash of colour, what will one find at the top of that hill? Time is forgotten. It is like a suspension of speed; and besides,' he finished, 'leaving for a walk is the only departure that is not really a departure; one leaves, but one does not go away.'

'All that doesn't alter the fact that it is nearly six o'clock. Quick march, you idle girl,' commanded the colonel, giving his niece rather a cold look.

Instead of obeying him, she sighed and put her hand on Louis Duville's shoulder. This bold gesture was followed by a moment of stupor, silence and immobility. Louis Duville smiled: 'You see,' he said, 'we are engaged.'

'Engaged!' Explain yourself!' cried the colonel.

Mme Duville, like a large bird pouncing on its prey, threw herself into her husband's arms and stammered: 'Engaged, did you hear? Engaged, like us!' Naïvety is more touching than beautiful, but she seemed beautiful in these simple words.

M. Duville's patience and goodness were accompanied by a touch of irony and a great deal of resignation. He knew that the less intelligent people are, the more easily they are hurt, having within them fewer remedies for pain. His wife often irritated him, but he was touched by her as she was good and well-meaning to a pathetic degree. It was therefore natural that she should love this husband whom she understood no better than on their first day together and who, by preserving her youthful illusions, had remained her fiancée after more than thirty years of marriage. Apart from her son and her husband, she felt real affection only for M. Zaraguirre. 'Engaged, like us!' she repeated, and embraced her husband instead of her son. The colonel shared in this moment of emotion and the following effusions. He was at the height of astonishment while M. and Mme Duville were at the height of happiness. There were exclamations, tears and kisses, the colonel praised his niece's family, and then they sat down and made plans.

'Let's get married at once,' suggested Louis Duville.

'At least give us time to turn round,' answered his mother.

M. Duville teased the engaged couple. 'Ah, you want to be married tomorrow so as to be alone together as soon as possible,' he told them. 'Lovers are always like that; they want solitude before everything else, and unfortunately they get it.' Mme Duville missed the point of this rather sad joke. 'Why are you laughing?' she asked them. 'This is hardly the moment.

Do you want to laugh or do you want to get married?' Then, addressing the girl, 'I do not approve of rushed marriages. They cause gossip and serve no good purpose, and I am sure your parents will agree with me. What a lot of preparations will have to be made! Marrying off a daughter is like moving house!'

The girl appeared distressed; she took her uncle aside and, speaking in a low voice, asked him to explain what was troubling her.

'This is very embarrassing,' began the colonel, 'for as soon as there is a question of sentiment, one finds oneself being melodramatic.'

'Sentiment and fog have a peculiar power,' said M. Duville; 'in both one gets lost, hears voices and tries to reach the others, but nobody can be found and yet everybody is there.'

'On the contrary, it is a meeting which my niece wishes to avoid. Call her childish or over-sensitive if you like, but she would rather not marry your son in the same church where she was married for the first time. I think it is understandable. Do you agree?'

'But you're not going to be married in Paris? Paris is nothing. Paris is a garage. The autumn is magnificent at Valronce, you must be married here,' cried Mme Duville, who then began to talk about receptions, announcements, music and hams. She decided that one ball and two dinner-parties should precede the marriage ceremony, the date of which she settled for Wednesday 22nd October, at midnight. 'The house will be full of the family, and we will take a floor at the Hotel Saint-Pépin for the guests who come from a distance. A month will soon be over,' she finished, 'what is a month, I ask you?'

M. Duville went to the library where he wrote a telegram to M. Zaraguirre: 'Louis marrying at Valronce 22nd October, we are happy, we expect you.'

The colonel took leave of his hosts, advising his niece not to return home too late, and Louis Duville took his fiancée to dine on the banks of the Saône. M. and Mme Duville remained alone at Valronce; they walked in the garden at night and passed the evening reminding each other of a whole series of memories both little and great.

* * *

The girl left the following day for the East of France, where her family lived. Louis Duville wanted to drive her there, but she refused: 'My parents have not such generous natures as yours, they have to be prepared for the least visit. If we arrive together, it will present them with *a fait accompli* and that will displease them. As it is, I shall have difficulty in making them understand how I could have decided to marry you, without knowing you.'

'I'm a bit like your parents,' Louis Duville replied. 'You should have prepared me for this abrupt departure. Why did you say nothing about it yesterday at dinner?'

'Yesterday? At dinner? We did nothing but look at each other in silence.'

They were lying in the shade of a tree in the colonel's garden. 'I come to spend the day with you and you receive me by saying goodbye? I arrive and you announce that you are leaving? You won't return, you will forget me, I'm sure of it.'

'Forget you? No, I no longer belong to myself, my life is in your hands and the idea of leaving you terrifies me.'

'Then you love me?' said Louis Duville.

'I love you, and if I have not come back in three days you will come and join me in the East.'

He drove her to the station, followed her on to the train and offered to accompany her to the end of her journey and wait for her in a village near her house.

'We live in the middle of the country, I haven't a car and wouldn't know how to come and find you; no, be reasonable and stay at Valronce.'

Louis Duville jumped on to the platform, she called out of the window something that he did not hear and, sad at heart, he returned to Valronce.

In the park at Valronce there was a little building, in the same style as the Orangerie, which was known as the Herbarium. This building contained the Duville family's collection of plants and many vegetable and mineral curiosities: samples of wood, stones, fossils and a library of botanical books. It consisted of a single room, long and mysterious, which smelt of dead leaves, cigars and paper. It was a sort of museum and laboratory where M. Duville spent his Sundays and his spare time. His wife, as a rule, did not go there. That day, she had come in and was watching him pressing some plants, when Louis Duville entered.

'What a face! What a sad lover!' said his father, laughing.

'She has gone,' answered Louis Duville.

'Gone? Already? What a catastrophe! Perhaps her uncle knows where she is! We simply must catch her,' cried Mme Duville.

She was in tears. Her son calmed her without, however, succeeding in reassuring himself, for his love gave him equal reasons to trust and to despair. His love affairs, till then, had been light-hearted and had only given him pleasure, but now he was uneasy.

The next day, as he was saying to his father, 'I think about her but cannot remember her – does that mean that she will have forgotten me?' he received a message from her which contained these words: 'Come, I am waiting for you.' He left.

Mme Duville profited by his absence to make arrangements. Helped by the servants at Valronce and seconded by Faneau, the butler, she drew up lists and inventories. All the cupboards were opened, linen was piled in the hall, glass and plate on the staircase and silver almost everywhere. 'If one wants order, one must have disorder first,' she said, and she shouted at the painters who were redecorating the apartment allotted to the future couple: 'Be quick! I don't want it to smell of paint. The smell of paint in the autumn is depressing. You can do it again in the spring.' Upholsterers were working in the ground-floor rooms; there was nowhere to sit and M. Duville took advantage of this state of affairs to linger either at the Herbarium or at his place of business.

Mme Duville organised dinner-parties at little tables, had the piano tuned, telegraphed for orchestras, hurried from the church to the confectioner and said to her husband: 'What we need above all on the 22nd is a full moon. That always makes a good effect.'

'Alas! I cannot alter the course of the stars,' he answered, 'and on the 22nd of October the moon will still be only in its first quarter.'

'Some people manage: it's quite simple, you have to pray. You are forgetting miracles!' she replied. M. Duville forgot them.

More than a week after his son's departure he received a letter from him dated from Paris, and by the same post a letter written by M. Zaraguirre from Amsterdam. 'I am happy for you, for Louis and for his mother,' he wrote. 'I congratulate you all. Is the fiancée pretty? I will arrive on the 20th and stay several days.'

As for Louis Duville, he described to his father how he had been received by his future parents-in-law. 'They are not like you and me. They are cold and formal and, although still young, seem to be old. They are thoroughly unpleasant and their son and his wife resemble them. You would not like them, Mother would drive them mad, and I pity their daughter who has lived with them for seven years and has been ceaselessly reproached for being a widow. If I do not dare to talk to you about her it is because you understand everything and then I would no longer have a secret. It seems that love cannot console her for her long unhappiness. She needs to be cherished and cared for like those dying plants which can only be revived by constant solicitude and which, when they flower at last, give one the double joy of conquest and charity.'

Louis Duville also told his dear father that he would have liked to bring his fiancée to Paris, so that she could buy clothes from the fashionable dressmakers, but her parents were against it. 'I have had her measurements taken and am choosing dresses for her myself. She will find them at Valronce. I have never enjoyed myself so much before in Paris.'

M. Duville read this letter to his wife. All the neighbourhood learnt from her that the bride would wear a tzigane dress of gold muslin with flounces, and the future wife, on hearing the same news, laughed to herself at the thought of her parents' expressions when she appeared wearing a dress from a private world.

Should it be said that this young woman had given her friends and relations some reason for keeping her at a distance? Her slow glances, the way she moved her head, the mantilla that she wore on Sundays and everything that her parents condemned as 'Spanish coquetry', had disturbed the peace of several happy households. It was doubtless to cheat loneliness and boredom that, apparently ignorant of the passions she aroused, she played a game of promising without compromising herself. There was even a suggestion of distance in the way she held out the flower of illusion like a sceptre. She was mistress of a reserve that made men dream, and women resented that. No one could reproach her for anything, and yet no one trusted her. However she had a heart and was capable of love.

Louis Duville did not return to Valronce until the 14th of October. His fiancée arrived on the morning of the 18th with her parents, her brother and her sister-in-law, and on the evening of the 20th M. Zaraguirre got out of his car, tall and handsome as the night and carrying presents. The double doors of the drawing-room were opened and he appeared, imposing, at his ease, his forehead lightly touched by the breath of adventure. Those who did not know him were conscious of the force of his presence. He greeted, embraced, kissed hands, and showed by each gesture that he felt at home, that his friends were dear to him and that he was happy to prove it. Prepared to like him, the girl loved him. He admired her, complimented her parents on having brought her into the world and congratulated Louis Duville on his beautiful conquest.

Dinner, that evening, only brought to Valronce the Duvilles and their son, his fiancée and her family, the colonel and M. Zaraguirre. The large, gay receptions prepared with so much care by the mistress of the house were not to start until the following day; none the less, to give this intimate dinner a festive air, she had lit the dining-room by candles. This flattered the appearance of the guests and softened the gloomy faces of the girl's parents. Outraged by the fact that their daughter had as yet received nothing more from Louis Duville than a modest gold and topaz ring, they regarded him with mistrust and suspected that he was less rich than he made out. Their attitude was a constraint on enjoyment; nobody spoke and the colonel was the first to break the silence by admiring the flowers that decorated the table: 'God!' he said.

'Yes, nature is the source of the greatest surprises,' said M. Zaraguirre. 'It confronts us with an imagination that surpasses our own.'

'The simplest flower defies the pretentions of men and their mechanical inventions,' M. Duville declared. 'Machines are born old, superseded, out of date, and, even in movement, they are inert, whereas motionless plants go through the ages with the authority and the speed of apparitions. There is nothing at the same time as new and as ancient as a flower.'

The colonel then remarked on the Japanese trees, which led him to talk about the Russo-Japanese war of 1902. Owing to his loquacity and the replies that it provoked, the first part of the dinner took on a certain animation which changed to real gaiety, when, before the dessert, Louis Duville rose and slipped a ruby ring on his fiancée's finger. Her eyes, which knew so well how to express love, were veiled with tears, and placing her hand on the table-cloth beside each of the guests in turn she went round the table repeating: 'Look!' Her family recognised in this gift the sign of a considerable fortune that would be shared by a young woman whom they had despised. Realising that the moment had come to be reunited with her and to cultivate her, they became more lively, their faces seemed to grow rounder and they shamelessly assumed the greatest affection for her.

Before dinner Louis Duville had shown M. Zaraguirre the engagement ring and other jewels that he intended to give his fiancée on the following day. 'She must have two surprises. Then we shall each have our moment,' M. Zaraguirre had told him. 'The little nonsense that I have brought for you is burning my fingers,' and, when they left the table, he presented the engaged couple with a tray carrying several jewel-boxes. 'Oh!' they cried, 'all that for us!'

M. Zaraguirre's presents were turquoises and diamonds set in gold. There were boxes, buttons, bracelets and brooches and, surpassing all these objects in beauty, there was a magnificent necklace formed by interlocking capital letters composing this sentence: 'The gods owe it to you, friendship gives it to you.' M. Zaraguirre's imagination, his expert taste and his delight in giving pleasure were illustrated by these jewels and gave them a value and a quality out of the common.

'Oh! What marvels! What marvels! It is beautiful! It is too beautiful! Thank you, thank you.'

She took the necklace and handed it to M. Zaraguirre. 'You must be the first,' she told him. Louis Duville and his father applauded this gesture. Then M. Zaraguirre placed the necklace on her neck and the click of the clasp could be heard.

'Your happiness is mine, be happy,' he told her.

Meanwhile the strains of unexpected music rose from the garden; the curtains were drawn and through the smoke of

Bengal lights four young men and four girls could be seen singing and playing the guitar and the violin. M. Duville opened the window: 'It is cold, come in,' he called. They pretended to have no other intention than to serenade the lovers, but really the young men were curious to know the woman for whom Louis Duville was renouncing celibacy, and the girls were only there for M. Zaraguirre. He liked their high spirits, their questions and their laughter; he became their friend; they surrounded him, he paid them attentions and the fiancée was jealous of them. When the young men took up their violins again, the girls took their guitars; everyone sat down to listen and the fiancée led M. Zaraguirre to a dark corner of the drawing-room. 'You remind me of an imaginary memory,' he told her.

'An imaginary memory? That is what you are for me,' she replied.

As he had attracted so many women by that mixture of presence and absence which contains the most dangerous allure, so in the same way he attracted her by a certain uncertainty,

that touch of the absolute which is called charm and is perhaps genius of the soul. She was fascinated by everything in him that was unattainable and, resenting the young musicians who knew how to amuse him, she already wanted to be his favourite.

'Yes, an imaginary memory,' she repeated, and he was charmed with her accent.

When the evening came to an end in long embraces, a presence haunted M. Zaraguirre's imagination, and after wishing the inhabitants of Valronce a good night he remained alone in the garden.

One can get drunk on dreams. He dreamed, then pulled himself together, explored his feelings and was indignant with himself. Gradually his heart grew calm. Although he was not capricious he decided that he had been the victim of a caprice which he had been able to see through, and, reassured, he climbed the steps to the house, turned out the lights and went up to his room.

* * *

Mme Duville had asked the colonel to invite his niece and her family to lunch the next day: 'Keep them at Dentelle as long as possible,' she had told him.

It was the day before the wedding. M. Duville and his son had to lunch in the town with M. Zaraguirre; no one would be at Valronce and so she would be free to devote herself to the final preparations for the evening.

M. Zaraguirre felt a certain remorse. The idea of having loved the girl appalled him; he was disgusted with himself and this disgust was reflected on her. 'How dare she attract me? That woman has no heart. If I love her, it's her fault. I would rather die than have anything to do with her,' he thought, and when he saw her again in the morning he felt no emotion. She was going out: 'I am going to Dentelle. One can love people without being entertained by them; I love my uncle but I am bored in his company. The days are long at Dentelle,' she told him. 'Why don't you come too and save me?'

'I will come,' answered M. Zaraguirre.

During lunch with the Duvilles he told them of this plan, which they could only approve, and when they returned to their office he left for Dentelle to join her.

It was his first visit, and the colonel showed him over the unused, well ordered house, hung with cotton materials of an oriental design that had been fashionable in the last century. Souvenirs of the First and Second Empires stood out against this bizarre background, and one could see the crossing of the Bérésina, the cavalry charge at Reichshoffen, Nils Forsberg's *The Grandfather and the Evil Tidings* next to drawings by George Scott and Bernard Naudiééén of soldiers in 1914. Military heroism, the spirit of sacrifice and fidelity to duty were honoured under this patriot's roof. M. Zaraguirre thought it very fine and the girl, who accompanied him from room to room, admired what he admired.

'Ah!' she said from time to time.

'Night is falling,' M. Zaraguirre told her, 'and I think we should go back.'

'At least wait for some chocolate and a brioche,' cried the colonel.

M. Zaraguirre did not want to disappoint him, and during the meal he talked of his travels with the fiancée's family. Nothing that he said was ordinary; he interested the men and greatly pleased the women, and everyone sighed when he rose to leave.

'You can't imagine how beautiful the countryside is here, my niece has no idea of it,' the colonel told him. 'Take her along the upper road; the panorama from there is superb, especially in autumn. From here to Valronce takes a little more than an hour. The only danger on that road is that one loiters on the way.'

His niece embraced him, M. Zaraguirre stood aside on the threshold to let her pass and all the family watched them as they got into the car.

They had scarcely left before M. Zaraguirre was tempted to take the girl back to her uncle. They did not speak but they understood each other and a current of passion passed through them both. Their thoughts and their confusion were the same and the same loyalty put them on their guard. They did not want to love each other. She heard the hubbub of her wedding and the buzzing of voices wishing her happiness. She turned her engagement ring on her finger, reminded herself of Louis Duville and believed that she still belonged to him.

M. Zaraguirre drove faster and faster so that their return journey assumed the nature of a flight, and when he took a turning without slowing down she gave a cry and was thrown against him. He stopped. 'You are frightened, forgive me.'

'Yes, yes, I was frightened, I thought I was going to die.'

'Die, what a pleasant word that is,' he said, and she looked at him. Their glances met, deepened and confessed the secret that their lips held back. Dismayed by this understanding, they nevertheless controlled themselves. 'Ah! then I am heartless!' she cried. At these words M. Zaraguirre drew her slowly to him and they remained for a moment in the chilly attitude of lovers who press close to each other as though they are cold.

They exchanged neither kisses nor words and arrived at Valronce before anyone else had returned.

M. Zaraguirre now saw no other remedy for his distress than to take possession of its cause.

* * *

Mme Duville had asked the fiancées to wait before making their appearance until all the guests were gathered in the drawing-rooms at Valronce, which had been converted into winter gardens, so that everyone could admire the handsome couple that they made. The girl came in on Louis Duville's arm. She wore a light grey dress and sparkled with the jewels that he had just given her. She was pale. He had said to her, 'You are more beautiful than ever,' and she had replied, 'It is love,' which made him happy. She would have liked to comfort him. 'Don't they suit each other well?' Mme Duville repeated, as she preceded them from group to group.

Everything at Valronce that evening – air, light, music, and the evidence of love – foretold happiness, promised joy, and encouraged pleasure; nothing marred the success of the party. The garden was illuminated and the colonel danced a tango. His niece's parents let themselves be carried away in a waltz and her brother and his wife sank into gaiety with that mixture of fear and audacity peculiar to dragon-flies. Couples intimately strolling together might find an orchestra of three musicians and a small buffet waiting for them at the Herbarium.

As much by his reputation as by his personal authority, M. Zaraguirre made several women dream, who believed themselves past temptation, and love reigned so completely over this evening that disappointed couples felt their hearts re-awaken. Mme Duville was in heaven. The girl kept as near as possible to Louis Duville and M. Zaraguirre did not ask her to dance. Yet when, during the dance, they passed close to each other by chance and inadvertently touched for a moment, they trembled and felt themselves on board a sinking ship.

The older people left on tiptoe, and when it was time for supper only the young, and those wise enough to set sleep aside for pleasure, remained. To the annoyance of the girls, Louis Duville asked M. Zaraguirre to his table and placed him beside his fiancée, who thus found herself between them both. The presence of other guests forced her to appear lively and prevented her from keeping M. Zaraguirre at a distance, but when they looked at each other they were carried away beyond their glances into the inexpressible, and they could not play at conversation.

After supper the ball assumed a more languid tone, and Louis Duville took his fiancée under the trees. His arm was round her waist and he was deeply moved.

'What a night,' she said. 'It is all so pretty, and your mother maintains that tomorrow it will be even prettier.'

'This time tomorrow we will be travelling, alone together, my love,' he answered.

'Ah! I am tired, tired,' she said, and as he brought her back to the house they met M. Duville who was out walking with M. Zaraguirre.

'We are going to the Herbarium, I believe no one has been there yet,' M. Duville told them. 'My wife is therefore right when

she says that my good ideas are bad. She knows what people like, and something that doesn't please everybody has no value in her eyes.'

'Oh!' said M. Zaraguirre. 'Caution is fruitless and the spirit of reason is of small account beside instinct. Instinct is the source of the great emotions; beauty is revealed by a physical disturbance and it is to that disturbance that we return. Our personal time, limited by our life, does not always allow us to reach the moment when we could appreciate things that belong essentially to an indefinite time.'

Mme Duville appeared on the steps and interrupted them. 'Ah! There you are! I was wondering where you had got to. Everyone is looking for you!' she cried.

'We are going to the Herbarium,' her husband replied.

'Leave the Herbarium where it is and come and look after your guests. They haven't come here to see me.'

Louis Duville indicated his fiancée languishing on his arm. 'See how pale and tired she is, she is nearly dead,' he said and he asked M. Zaraguirre to take her to the Herbarium. 'She can rest there, wait for us,' added M. Duville, and the girl, supported by M. Zaraguirre, disappeared under the trees.

In the Herbarium, the candles were low and three musicians were dozing in the long room where nothing had been tidied.

Large books and piles of papers cluttered up the tables, and shrubs placed round the room mingled their scent with the mystery of botanical studies and the smell of books and collections of plants. She stopped by the small buffet, took some fruit, asked the musicians to eat and drink and said: 'Will you play *Harlequin's Millions* for me?' M. Zaraguirre, leaning against a pedestal which supported a bust of Buffon, watched her and waited for her in the shadows. She rejoined him as one returns to the person one loves, with that inspired look and step that love sometimes gives to women, and they sat down at a distance from the orchestra on a slightly raised bench, behind a high desk.

'You are unhappy, aren't you?' M. Zaraguirre said.

'I am desperate. You see, it was chance that brought me to Valronce where everything is so attractive and beautiful. I laughed with Louis Duville behind my uncle's back and that drew us together. He is charming, he charmed me and I wanted the happiness he offered me. It is understandable that I should be delighted by so simple a prospect, and I loved Louis, yes, I loved

him and I love him still with all my heart. Tell me, have I confused love with affectionate friendship, or am I really heartless?'

She was touching, sincere and in great distress.

'Friendship is often as sudden as love,' answered M. Zaraguirre. 'Friendship is a wise form of love that reassures the heart and doesn't disturb the imagination.'

'Ah! I don't want to lie to Louis or to deceive him, yet that is what I am doing when I realise that in the future I shall do nothing else. My life was blameless before you came but since you are here everything has changed, even myself.'

She bent her head and began to cry. 'I am lost, lost, I think of you too much,' she went on, making a gesture as though to tear out her heart.

M. Zaraguirre raised her face towards his. 'You are crying for a sorrow which I am the last to wish to console. I love you,' he told her.

'Ah!' she said, and they embraced.

The great passion of first kisses baffles reason. It is the sky in the tomb, a deep falling. Anyone who has not experienced it will remain censorious for ever.

When they recovered themselves, heavy with fervour and dismay, she passed the back of her hand across her lips and then lent her palm against M. Zaraguirre's mouth. The violinist came up and asked them what they would like to hear. M. Zaraguirre requested *In Mir Klingt Ein Lied* and they left the shadows, helped themselves to wine, exchanged glasses and went to sit by a red curtain, among the shrubs, near the orchestra. M. Zaraguirre lit a cigar: 'We must tell the truth,' he declared.

'The truth? Never. It is too late. I haven't the courage to cause so much pain, I would rather die, and tomorrow I shall be on my honeymoon.'

'With me,' replied M. Zaraguirre.

A moment later M. Duville came in with his son and several young people who wished to take leave of the future bride.

M. Zaraguirre interrupted the good nights: 'We haven't danced together yet,' he said to the girl, and while M. Duville blew out the candles and the orchestra played a drowsy waltz he led her off and whispered in her ear: 'I love you, you are driving me mad, I adore you.' Louis Duville heard the murmur but not the sense of these words.

In the night, still very dark, the garden already smelled of the dawn. M. Duville shut the door of the Herbarium and they slowly returned to the house. The drawing-rooms at Valronce were empty; the last guests left with the musicians: the party was over.

Louis Duville detained his fiancée in the hall. He asked her if she had enjoyed herself, if she were happy and if she loved him. She told him that she had spent the most beautiful evening of her life. 'Come,' he said, opening his arms to her, but instead of throwing herself into them she turned aside, so that he had to beg her, and when she finally embraced him he found no trace on her lips of her usual ardour. Her kisses had changed their meaning.

'You don't really love me tonight,' he said.

'Don't say that, please! One can love and be tired, and I am tired; try to understand.'

'No, it is something else. I feel that I irritate you or that you are hiding something from me. You are not the same. Has someone annoyed you or upset you?'

'No, no one. There is nothing the matter, I promise. Let us go to bed, it is late, and we have not much time.'

'My darling, my love, tell me again that you are happy and that you love me.'

'What can I say except that you are worrying for no reason? You *are* worried, why?'

'Tell me what Zaraguirre whispered in your ear while you were dancing.'

'He was humming the words of the waltz.'

'Were they words of love?'

'I don't know, it was in German.'

'Is that true?'

'But, you are jealous! Jealous of him! So that's what has annoyed you. I would scold you if I had the strength.'

'If he were not our friend – and what a friend! – I would be right to fear him. He has every quality that might make you prefer him to me, and, what is more, his indifference is attractive.'

'You think him indifferent?'

'Why do you ask me that?'

'Because he interests me,' she said, yawning.

The frankness of this reply reassured Louis Duville. His love and his pride were gratified. 'There is no one more interesting. Come,' he said, 'you are dying of sleep,' and happy again, he took her to her room.

The fiancée removed her jewels and put them back in their boxes. She undressed, put on her nightdress and dressing-gown

and with her hair loose leant on the balcony of her window. Too honest to look for excuses, too good to be happy, but too much in love to be rational, she stayed there, not thinking, overwhelmed by the weight of what had happened between the future and the past. Suddenly, mingling with the creaking of branches moved by the gentle breeze that often precedes the dawn, she heard the noise of a door being slowly opened below. She leant out. It was M. Zaraguirre. He was carrying two suitcases and was wearing a grey suit with a scarf tied round his neck. She thought that he was leaving. Governed by instinct rather than feeling, she ran downstairs, crossed the kitchen garden and joined him as he reached the coach-house.

'Go away,' she said, 'yes, leave me, abandon me.'

'Go away? Leave you here? What good do you think that would do? Abandon you when I love you? And bring about your unhappiness, my own and also your husband's? I would be mad to do such a thing.'

'Then where are you going?'

He took the coach-house key which hung from a nail on an ivy-covered wall and put his luggage in his car. Then he looked at the sky and foretold fine weather.

They returned to the house with their arms round each other. She was trembling and all strength had left her; that night they remained together.

At ten o'clock in the morning they left Valronce. Everyone was still asleep except for Louis Duville and his father who were at their office. M. Zaraguirre was silent and the girl, pressing herself close to him, moaned. He stopped a short way from the Duvilles' place of business: 'I am going to leave you alone for a moment. Ask me nothing. Wait,' and, ignoring the gesture that she made to hold him back, he left her and went straight up to Louis Duville's office. 'M. Louis only looked in this morning and I shall not see him again,' the secretary told him. 'Just think,

M. Zaraguirre, today is the great day! This evening we will all be at the wedding.'

M. Zaraguirre then went to find M. Duville, who was reading his letters: 'I really want to talk to Louis, but he is out and I can't wait,' he said.

'What are you in such a hurry about? Sit down.'

M. Zaraguirre did not move. 'Listen,' he began, 'you know how great a friendship binds me to all three of you? You will never doubt that? Each word that I am about to say pierces my heart.'

M. Duville went up to him. 'I am listening,' he said.

'I have come to tell you,' went on M. Zaraguirre, 'that this evening your son must not marry a woman who feels nothing but friendship for him.'

'Friendship? What an idea! What do you know about it?'

'I do know.'

'You do know? Very well, then, tell me how you know.'

'I know and I repeat that this evening Louis must not marry a woman who no longer loves him enough.'

'A woman who no longer loves him and whom you love yourself, is that it?'

'Yes,' answered M. Zaraguirre. 'I love her. She has left Valronce and is going away with me.'

'Go away,' shouted M. Duville, 'go away, leave this place! Go away and nurse your misery and remorse and leave us to cure our pain.'

They separated immediately and M. Duville banged the door on the heels of his friend.

The blow that M. Duville had just received touched him personally and wounded him still more cruelly in his affection for his son and Mme Duville. From what heights of happiness were they going to fall! They would suffer so greatly from the loss of their illusions. Knowing that his son had business at the town hall in the village of Valronce, where the civil wedding was to have taken place that afternoon, he hurried there to find him.

As his state of mind betrayed itself on his face, Louis Duville guessed at once that he brought bad news. 'Why have you come? What has happened?' he asked.

'Come, I must talk to you,' said his father; then without preparation he repeated each of M. Zaraguirre's words.

'No, it's impossible,' said Louis Duville. 'I don't believe it.'

It was nearly midday when they returned to Valronce. From the hall they heard the harmonious sound of scrubbing-brushes being passed by a team of workers over the drawing-room floors. The house smelled of lavender, encaustic paint and the wood fires that had just been lit in the downstairs rooms. Louis Duville and his father went up to the first floor and stopped outside his fiancée's door at the moment when her brother and sister-in-law came out of their room. 'Sh!' they said, 'she's asleep.'

'It is time to wake her,' answered Louis Duville.

He knocked once, twice, waited, knocked again, and went in followed by his father, while the young couple, who thought this behaviour highly unconventional, went off whispering to each other.

The bed had not been slept in and the jewel-boxes were open on the dressing-table; at the sight of the engagement ring Louis Duville could not control his feelings. 'Look, look!' he said. 'Then it's true? Oh! It's too unjust, it's too cruel; I loved her. I still love her and it's him that I blame. If he had let me see her again I could have convinced her, I know, and whatever he says I am sure that she loved me.' He paused and then added: 'I will have my revenge if I can.' M. Duville ascribed these words to the rancour and despair which his son must naturally feel, and advised him to leave Valronce. 'Go to Paris. I will look after your mother. Here you will suffer too much, and too many things will make you suffer.'

'What an insult! What do they think I am? Is there a worse humiliation than this?' 'The sorrows of love are always humiliating. They are caused by rejection or desertion, and any being or any thing that is deserted is pitiable.'

Louis Duville embraced his father. 'You are good, you are so good that you pity me. Yes, pity me, but don't let me see it, and don't let anybody talk to me again about this business. You are right, I will hide. Goodbye,' he said, and he went away.

M. Duville took the jewel-boxes to his wife. 'Prepare to cry,' he began. 'I find it hard not to weep.' She interrupted him. 'What have you got there?' she asked.

'The jewels. Pick out the ones from Louis and never let him see them again. As for the others, we will send them back. The engagement is broken off. We must cancel the wedding and will receive nobody tonight.'

'Cancel the wedding? Are you mad? It's impossible!'

'The engagement is broken off, do you understand?'

'Where is Louis? Go and find him.'

'Louis is now on his way to Paris.'

'Louis gone? Has he run away? What a catastrophe! How horrible! And the poor little thing? Has she given you back the jewels already? Where is she? What did she say? Say something, answer me, can't you see that I am going mad?'

The idea that her son could have been deserted never entered Mme Duville's mind. Her husband made her sit down. 'It was not he who broke off the engagement, it was she.'

'She? How can that be? Tell me.'

'It was like this,' he said, and he told her what had happened.

Mme Duville listened to her husband without interrupting, then her despair broke out like a sob long held back. She abused the unfaithful girl, her family and M. Zaraguirre; she gesticulated, moaned and wept. 'My poor Louis, he was so happy! No, no, it's too much. His future! Oh, my poor Louis. Everything was so nice!' she repeated through her tears. 'Help me get rid of those people!' M. Duville let her give vent to all her feelings, which he shared: he was in despair.

The fiancée's family were driven to the station and miserably took their departure. M. and Mme Duville sent messages and telegrams of cancellation to the church, the tradesmen and the guests, and when several people whom they had been unable to reach arrived at Valronce at dinner-time, thinking themselves expected, they were received by Faneau at the foot of the steps and told that the marriage would not take place and that they would find a meal prepared for them at the Hotel Saint-Pépin.

Late that night, M. Zaraguirre and the girl arrived at a hotel in Menton. The boldness of their act reinforced the bonds that already held them together. It is impossible to say whether or not they were happy, but it is certain that they were depending on time to dim the memory of the emotional disaster caused by their elopement.

This event made a great stir in the neighbourhood. All the Duvilles' friends shared their disappointment and no voice was raised in defence of the runaway couple. The colonel, who could not forgive himself for having, in all innocence, brought his niece to Valronce, and who was appalled by her scandalous conduct, let some time pass before daring to visit the Duvilles and offer his excuses and his condolence. Mme Duville overwhelmed him with reproaches which he bore without flinching. 'When you think that happiness is within your reach and it escapes you, you never recover! Why did you bring that devil into our lives?'

'I did not know her.'

'Then why was she staying with you?'

'She was my nephew's widow; I knew no more of her than that. But you knew your friend Zaraguirre well . . .'

'It is the people we know best who surprise us the most,' remarked M. Duville. 'What is done is done. We must force ourselves to forget it, and think only of the future.'

While they talked thus, Louis Duville's fiancée, who was now called Mme Zaraguirre, was sailing to South America and sleeping in her husband's arms. 'Think only of the future,' were the very words spoken by M. Zaraguirre to his wife as they boarded the ship which now carried their embrace. He hid his regrets from her. If he refused to look back it was because he could not remember Valronce without pain, the house, the Duvilles and all the memories of a lost friendship. His wife was the only person left to him in the world; he knew that he was her only happiness; he was sad against his will.

Louis Duville returned to his parents after a month and life at Valronce was resumed as it had been in the past.

Part Two

Business obliged M. Zaraguirre to travel and occasionally took him to wild districts where his wife could not follow him. As soon as they arrived in South America they settled in the town, in a sort of small palace that appeared to be built of sugar on a large promenade by the sea-shore. They had spent two months there before M. Zaraguirre had to leave for several days. His wife complained loudly and declared that she would see no one in his absence. M. Zaraguirre was pleased. He had not forgotten how she had forsaken Louis Duville, and although he had enjoyed all the advantages of that desertion he did not trust her and considered her capable of infidelity. On the eve of his departure he offered to drive her to a country house built in the colonial style which he had bought twenty years before and furnished in the old local tradition. Mme Zaraguirre took an immediate fancy to this house, which was called Tijo. 'I want to live here,' she said. 'I feel at home here, it is my house.' The walls of the hall and dining-room were covered by white earthenware tiles on which blue designs sometimes repeated the same pattern and sometimes depicted great naval scenes or vast landscapes. In the drawing-rooms, which were whitewashed in lime, rows of candles in silver sticks lit Dutch pictures and mirrors in thick ebony frames; the windows were hung with double curtains of white muslin and pale-blue watered silk which also covered the chairs of black jacaranda wood. Most of the objects at Tijo were silver, including the baths and even the tubs containing rose laurels, lemon-trees and climbing plants entwined round bamboo poles. In the middle of the drawing-room a circular sofa, upholstered in plush with an oriental pattern, surrounded a cluster of tree-fern reminiscent of the famous garden of Montserrat, at Cintra near Lisbon. For M. Zaraguirre the plants were always wild; he called them 'My little savages' and the rarest at Tijo were presents from M. Duville and came from Valronce. That was why since his marriage M. Zaraguirre had not wanted to return to this house where the memory of his greatest friend would be forced on him when he wished to set it aside. When he confessed this to Mme Zaraguirre she shrugged her shoulders. 'One cannot mourn for ever. Thank God, we are far away from Valronce,' she said, and her answer displeased

M. Zaraguirre. After dinner that evening they lay side by side on a large chaise-longue in the patio. M. Zaraguirre held a fan which he moved from time to time; he did not speak and was smoking a cigar.

'What are you thinking about?' his wife asked him.

'I was thinking about the Herbarium and the time we spent there on our last night at Valronce.'

'Ah!' she said, 'You are not all mine. I am jealous of your regrets.'

'Regrets fight against reason,' he said, 'thereby compelling us to notice them.'

Mme Zaraguirre sat up. 'Listen,' she said, 'I loved the Duvilles, yes, I loved them, but now I hate them, do you hear? We have hurt them and that is terrible, but what can one do, in life everyone ends by being hurt in some way or another. I cannot open a newspaper without reading stories of people killing themselves for love, so why should I feel sorry for the Duvilles? They have their business, their money, their health and the consolation of being victims. What more do they need? I ask you! It is I who should be pitied, not they. You make me responsible for what has happened and you resent me as though it were my fault that you have lost your beloved Duvilles. And I may say that. . .'

'That is enough!' M. Zaraguirre interrupted. 'You are depressing me and you are in danger of making me angry. Be a cross and jealous child if you will, but if you are a heartless woman don't let me see it. Stop destroying your reasons for being happy and remember that I have a horror of complaints and recriminations.'

He rose, threw away his cigar which shot out sparks of flame, and disappeared. Mme Zaraguirre also rose, stamped her foot, shouted, called him and went back to the house where, followed by the servants, she looked for him in vain. He had left on his journey. She learnt her lesson and wept. Her lady's maid, a fat negress, helped her to bed, put a pile of handkerchiefs on her bedside table and fanned her face until she fell asleep. The days of solitude, anxiety and sadness which succeeded that evening kept her at Tijo. She admitted her faults and feared that she had lost her attraction; she waited for M. Zaraguirre but dreaded seeing him again. On his return he found her contrite which reassured him, strengthened his affection and gave him new excuses for spoiling her. From now on when he spoke of Valronce without hiding his regrets she listened with a smile which suggested that she shared in his nostalgia.

Mme Zaraguirre was fairly intelligent but she was not intellectual. This pleased her husband. 'Intellect spoils the sweetness of women, makes them unnatural and pretentious and chills love. Intellect interferes with desire,' he said. What he liked in women were their feet, their hands, an unusual smile, a way of playing, a palpitation, coquetry, scent. He gradually made his wife the woman he loved and she made him the happiest of men. He overwhelmed her with presents; he was proud of displaying her and the more she was admired the more he loved her, as though the attention paid her by others renewed his love, changed

its form, strengthened its passion and increased the privileges of intimacy. Their union attracted interest. M. Zaraguirre's age and stature set off the youth of his wife, who looked like his daughter and whom he treated as his mistress. People fought over them, their presence ensured the success of any social occasion and Mme Zaraguirre, while retaining her provincial simplicity and the air of a young tennis-playing girl, grew conscious of her position, gained confidence and soon became an object of snobbery. She reigned over Tijo and organised a life there similar to the one she would have lived in the country in France. She loved animals, the poultry yard and the kitchen garden; she was seen to milk the cows, collect the eggs and personally tend her husband's favourite plants. She founded a dispensary and taught little girls to embroider. Wearing a large straw hat, a white blouse and a pleated black sateen skirt, she rode to the local markets where a simple and colourful world looked on her as a queen. She enjoyed this, and often went for twilight drives in a carriage drawn by two white horses imported from Europe. Birds that she had tamed fluttered around her and perched on her shoulders or her head. Proud of her conquest and the honour they paid her, she called them 'My compliments'. When M. Zaraguirre returned to Tijo at

dinner-time and found her wearing a flowing dress of white lawn with blue bows and little blue satin pumps, he kissed her and told her: 'You smell blue.' Attracted by the modesty that gives abandon its value, he admired his wife's reserved appearance and forbade her to wear pink and above all pink under-linen which he considered the height of vulgarity. 'The eloquence of pink is shocking,' he said. When they were alone in the evening he read to her while she did needlework, and on Sundays they asked their friends to informal dinner-parties. On those nights guitarists played and sang in the drawing-rooms and on the patio; everyone got a little drunk, and while the men ardently courted the mistress of the house, the women surrounded M. Zaraguirre, drew him apart and flattered themselves with the hope that one day he would be unfaithful. There, as elsewhere, his presence dominated the evening.

Thus they lived in the most tender harmony. M. Zaraguirre travelled frequently but always alone, for his wife refused to leave Tijo, even to go to Europe which he visited five times in five years. These separations, far from dividing them, on the contrary drew them together by the opportunities they gave them to cherish each other and embrace in thought, as at the start of their beautiful love.

Mme Zaraguirre often heard from her parents and her brother without M. Zaraguirre asking what their letters contained:

'They approve of my having preferred you to Louis Duville,' she had told him at the beginning of their marriage, and since then he had despised them. Time had not changed his feelings: he missed Valronce.

As for M. Duville, he was inconsolable, and it was loyalty to his son that prevented him from writing to M. Zaraguirre. 'What is the point of this quarrel? Pride spoils everything,' he said privately to the young women who missed his friend as he did. October at Valronce had become the saddest month in the year.

One day M. Zaraguirre said to his wife: 'I have to go to Europe. I have a lot to do in France and I don't like that. I am always depressed there.'

'I will come with you,' she said. 'Tijo is my real home, as you know, but if I never make up my mind to move my parents will end by believing that you have isolated me. When are you leaving?'

'In two weeks from now.'

They embarked in August. Mme Zaraguirre was not a good sailor and from the start of the journey she was also homesick for her house, her animals, her garden and everything that she had left behind her.

Her husband tried to interest her in the character of the different countries that they had occasion to visit. 'There are so many beautiful things I want to show you,' he said.

'Ah!' she replied, 'London, Hamburg and Marseilles do not tempt me, and I confess that I would rather go straight to my family than drag myself round big cities. You will be busy, I shall scarcely see you and you will be surrounded by people who speak a language I do not understand.'

'What do you mean? I will certainly find time to go out with you, to take you to theatres and museums . . .'

'Ah! Museums are dead, I don't like them; and besides, our pictures at Tijo are enough for me. No, I shall go to the East of

France and you will come and fetch me there. I know that my parents will be happy to see you.'

'I am not going to the East of France, I have nothing to do there, I know no one and should be bored, but I will wait for you at Menton where we can stop before going home.'

'At Menton! Ah, yes. I like that idea. Do you remember Menton?'

'I remember,' he said.

On arrival in England M. Zaraguirre took his wife on board another boat; he placed her in the captain's care and she left for Ostend where her parents were staying.

They gave her the warmest welcome, flattered her and congratulated her on having married a man who was certainly richer and more attractive than Louis Duville had been. She accompanied them to the East of France and confided in them: 'Yes, I am happy, perhaps too happy, it would be difficult to be more so, and yet there is a shadow on my happiness.'

'A shadow? What shadow?' her mother asked. 'Perhaps you regret not having children.'

'Children? No, it's not that.'

'Well, then, what shadow can you mean?'

'Men are strange, they are really fond of each other! Love is not strong enough to defeat friendship. My husband is faithful to his memories and regrets the circumstances of our marriage. "Love can only defeat love" is what he says, and it is a bit cruel, isn't it?'

She was pitied and admired. The size of her luggage, her generosity and the prestige of her position caused a sensation. She saw her room again, kissed her doll and relived the life of her years of widowhood; she did not try to please others as her love for M. Zaraguirre removed the desire. After six weeks, proud of her importance, she bade her family a farewell full of promises and left to join her husband at Menton. She arrived there in the evening. He was waiting for her at the station, and he carried rather than led her to the hotel where, five years ago, they had lived from the night of their flight to the morning of their marriage. In the same rooms filled with the same flowers they recovered intact the mood of escape and the rhythm and taste of their past embraces.

They attracted attention. At thirty Mme Zaraguirre was still graced with the charms of her early youth and M. Zaraguirre, in his early sixties, carried his years with an increasing brilliance as a legend grew around his name. Their entrance at a restaurant caused a moment of silence and, while all eyes followed them from the door to the table where they were to sit, forks hung suspended between plates and mouths. There was no one there who did not long to approach them, in order to boast about it later certainly, and even more to enjoy the pleasant atmosphere with which a vast and romantic fortune surrounded them.

It was at Menton that M. and Mme Zaraguirre met Mme Dajeu who was resting there under doctor's orders. Highly informed as to the value of certain connections, she was the centre in Paris of a circle of rich industrialists, although not herself a Parisian. In the business world her husband had had occasion to dine with M. Zaraguirre whom he admired and cited as an example. She therefore had, she considered, good reasons for making herself known to him, and one afternoon, while M. and Mme Zaraguirre were having tea in the hotel garden, she approached them, simpering, and said: 'I have so often heard you spoken of that I feel I know you'; she then mentioned her husband's name.

'Dajeu? Sugar?' asked M. Zaraguirre.

'Exactly, sugar, that's us,' she answered, and M. Zaraguirre invited her to dinner.

The ladies got on wonderfully well together. They discussed travel, novels and fashion, and Mme Dajeu declared that the wind was a menace to her *coiffure*. She could not bear open cars. Mme Zaraguirre, on the contrary, liked them: 'With a shawl one can manage,' she said; 'the air is so stimulating that it makes one forget everything, and my husband will tell you that speed is a wind that one can regulate at will. That is certainly worth a sacrifice.'

'A sacrifice? I don't understand,' said Mme Dajeu.

'Think of it like this. Speed and a hat don't go together. One must give up one or the other.'

'Speed and a hat! What a picture!'

'My husband,' Mme Zaraguirre went on, 'prefers trains to motor cars. It's incredible, isn't it?'

'The carriages, the sleepers, the freedom of movement within the greater movement of the train, yes, that I find altogether admirable,' said M. Zaraguirre. 'The train is the most poetic means of transport on earth and it can be the scene of strange encounters. One can choose between a caravan life, a drawing-room life or a life of love. As to the engine, in my view it is the most human and the most savage of machines; it gasps and pants like a living being, like a messenger who is running away, pursued by time, and goes from towns to villages delivering a share of presence, indifference and forgetfulness.'

'You see,' Mme Zaraguirre concluded, 'my husband adores engines.'

The following morning the two ladies walked together in the pretty streets of Menton. They went shopping.

'Who dresses you in Paris?' Mme Dajeu asked Mme Zaraguirre.

'In Paris? Me? Nobody. In Paris? I have never even been there.'

'*You*, never been to Paris? But what an injustice! And have you never complained?'

If Mme Dajeu wished only to be agreeable and was incapable of treachery, she was none the less highly ambitious and the fame of M. Zaraguirre dazzled her. She dreamed of attaching herself to a household whose friendship would add greatly to her personal prestige, and she pursued this dream in flattering and sympathising with Mme Zaraguirre: 'A woman like you far from Paris! What an injustice!' she repeated. Then Mme Zaraguirre described her life at Tijo: 'We get newspapers from

Paris, the literary and illustrated reviews. We are not savages, you see,' she said.

They had just entered a shop and were choosing scarves that a tradesman spread before them on the counter. They took them one by one, unfolded them and tied them round their necks, looking at themselves in the glass.

'Pink for Madame?' the shopkeeper suggested to Mme Zaraguirre.

'No, thank you, I never wear pink.'

'You never wear pink? Superstition?' asked Mme Dajeu.

'No. My husband doesn't like pink.'

'He doesn't like pink? How curious. Pink is so flattering, so soft, so feminine. But what is the good of discussing it? Old people have their own ideas and your husband is a wonderful old gentleman. He is unique. You don't find people like him any more.'

'He is wonderful, but he is not old,' replied Mme Zaraguirre, laughing.

They bought some scarves, idled at shop windows, and finally stopped at a pastry-cook's.

'It is true that friendship is as sudden as love,' Mme Zaraguirre remarked. 'I saw you for the first time yesterday and I know already how sorry I shall be to leave you. I have no French friends at Tijo.'

'How nice you are! If you come to Paris I shall be angry if you do not stay with me. Your husband knows who we are and our house may not be a palace but it is quite comfortable. So make up your mind to come. Alas, time holds nothing good in store for pretty women, and if I were in your place I should be inconsolable at having to spend the best years of my life at the end of the world between my kitchen garden and my linen cupboards. You don't know what you are missing. Your husband hides you; I can understand that. You are young and charming, and a mixture of selfishness and jealousy is natural in a man of his age who has had a good life and knows women only too well.'

'Selfish? Jealous? He? You are wrong. We would go to Paris tomorrow if I wished.'

'Well, then, what are you waiting for? Come and you will have all Paris at your feet. I go so far as to say that it is your right.'

'All Paris at my feet? You exaggerate, I am sure.'

Mme Dajeu insisted; she repeated her invitation and Mme Zaraguirre, seduced by banal images and promises of success, suddenly felt alarm at the flight of time and saw herself deprived of something that it was urgent to grasp. On returning from her walk she hurried to her husband who was reading under a tree: 'Let us go to Paris,' she said, 'the Dajeus have invited us.'

'They are very good, very serious and very boring people, and Mme Dajeu is an idiot, if I am not mistaken,' answered M. Zaraguirre.

'An idiot? Not at all, for as I have told you she has asked us to stay.'

'Stay with the Dajeus? No, thank you, I prefer a hotel. But, tell me, how is it that you are cured, as though by a miracle, of your horror of big cities?'

'As though by a miracle, exactly! Are you pleased?'

'I am pleased that you are giving me an opportunity to make you happy. You want to go to Paris? Very well, we will go.'

'Tomorrow?'

'No. Our fortune is not a gold ingot that has merely to be hidden. My business affairs involve other responsibilities and you know that the further a fortune extends the more it is in danger: it is like a dispersing army. I am expected at home and we must go back. However, I promise that we will return to France as soon as possible.'

Mme Zaraguirre made a grimace: 'As soon as possible, that is not a date, it might mean in two years, in ten years, how can one tell?'

'What do you want exactly?' M. Zaraguirre asked her.

'I love Tijo, it is a paradise, but it is a paradise at the end of the world. Is that true, yes or no? I am young, I would like to have a little fun, I deserve it, I even have a right to it. Mme Dajeu was telling me just now that the future holds nothing in store for pretty women: one fades and then it is too late.'

'What do you want exactly?' M. Zaraguirre repeated.

'Put yourself in my place. One only lives once and I am losing all my best years . . .'

'With me?'

'Oh! No, my love, not with you, but far away, at Tijo, between my kitchen garden and my linen cupboards.'

M. Zaraguirre no longer smiled: 'Explain yourself,' he said.

'I have nothing to explain. I have said it all, darling: I have been invited and, since you cannot put off your departure, allow me to spend a fortnight with the Dajeus. God knows when we will return. One might be ill. One might die. And then? I shall have got no further. Two weeks! I shall leave France on the day that you arrive home, and we will be together again for Christmas. You have left me so often! You must be used to our little separations, aren't you?'

'I have never had to make so difficult a choice,' replied M. Zaraguirre. 'I must go. If I make you come with me, you will be unhappy; you will rebel; I shall have forced you to act against your will, and our love can only suffer. You will think I have bullied you, you will resent me and at Tijo you will only find reasons to pity yourself and see yourself as a victim. Well, I hate complaints, I value our love and want to do nothing to endanger it.'

M. Zaraguirre thought that his wife would change her mind and that the surest method of making her consider was not to contradict her. 'Why should I not yield to your first whim?' he said. 'Go to Paris, then, if it makes you happy.'

Mme Zaraguirre clapped her hands: 'Thank you, darling, I adore you. You will really let me?'

'Really,' he replied.

She kissed him and petted him; she was happy, and yet her husband's unmoved and gentle manner, his air of detachment, caused her at the same time remorse and vexation: 'Does it mean nothing to you that I am leaving you? You won't forget me, at least?'

'Forget you? You?'

'If you tell me that I am hurting you, I shall go back with you.'

'You would hurt me much more by accompanying me and regretting it. If I forced you you would no longer love me. No, no, what is decided is decided: go to Paris.'

'If you insist,' she said.

'No, I don't insist.'

'A fortnight.'

'If you insist,' he replied.

M. Zaraguirre could not have wished for a better chaperon for his wife than Mme Dajeu. He knew it and thanked her for her invitation. He seemed sincere and gave her a box of chocolates.

Three days later, Mme Zaraguirre cried at leaving him. 'If you are sad, come with me,' he whispered: but as she continued to cry, he added: 'Enjoy yourself, that is my only wish.'

'And you, don't be bored.'

'I? Bored? I shall scarcely have time,' he answered, and a moment later, while he left by car for Genoa, Mme Dajeu and Mme Zaraguirre took the train to Paris.

* * *

On the journey Mme Dajeu tried to ease Mme Zaraguirre's conscience and to temper the pain that she felt at the idea of being separated from her husband. In spite of her efforts, she could not convince her of the innocence of an act that M. Zaraguirre had encouraged, nor could she dispel the sadness of a heart bent on exploring the sorrows of absence. Mme Zaraguirre reproached herself ceaselessly and Mme Dajeu, growing impatient, thought her absurd and regretted having invited her.

M. Dajeu was dining out that evening. His car met the travellers at the station and they found in it a bouquet and a welcoming note addressed to Mme Zaraguirre. These flowers given her by a stranger had the power to distract her, to awaken her little imagination and carry her thoughts towards the future. M. Dajeu returned home as they were arriving. He inquired about their journey and asked Mme Zaraguirre for news of her husband. She thanked him for the flowers that she held in her arms, and as his only answer was to mutter and cough she decided that this man did not interest her.

The Dajeus' drawing-room was an ultimate expression of the taste of newly rich industrialists at the peak of their social ambition. 'How beautiful it is!' said Mme Zaraguirre. She had never seen anything like it, and Mme Dajeu was amazed that M. Zaraguirre had not brought to South America from Paris the elements of a décor that was, in her view, the inevitable background to the best people.

Mme Dajeu took Mme Zaraguirre to her room whose windows looked on to the Bois de Boulogne. 'Tomorrow I shall introduce you to some of our friends. There will be some broken hearts,

there's no doubt about that.' They embraced, wishing each other good night, and Mme Dajeu retired. Mme Zaraguirre placed the photograph of her husband on her bedside table, went to bed, sighed and slept.

Her first day in Paris was to hold a surprise. She spent the morning going from Notre-Dame to the Louvre and in the late afternoon she could be seen in Mme Dajeu's drawing-room, surrounded by admirers sitting on cushions at her feet. She had retained the air of adolescence and charmed easily, less by self-confidence than by a desire to please. The unexpected is never conventional. An accent changes everything. Mme Zaraquirre had not had a chance before to hear a concert of Parisian voices and, out of her element, she took refuge from her shyness in laughter. A mirror between two windows showed her a reflection to which she turned for reassurance, and in this mirror she suddenly saw a man appear and approach her, whom she saw full-face although her back was turned to him. She rose, broke the circle of her admirers and ran to a door. Louis Duville reached her as she was going out, put his hand on her shoulder and held her. She did not turn round. 'Why are you running away?' he asked. She shook her head without replying.

'We must not make ourselves conspicuous. Stay. Memory survives but time soothes the heart. I forgave you a long time ago.'

'Ah! We would have been so happy if we had known that,' she said, turning to face him.

'You rejected the offer I made for your happiness and since then discretion has prevented me from contributing towards it. Let us forget all that. You are here, I am seeing you, I want to see you again; will you lunch with me?'

Their conversation apart had attracted Mme Dajeu's attention: 'How do you know each other, you sly people?' They pretended to be childhood friends and went to mingle with the other guests. Mme Zaraguirre was all the more attractive for being happier, and the broken circle formed itself around her once more. It was not the flattery of which she was the object that made her radiantly gay but rather the hope that Louis Duville would renew the links between Valronce and M. Zaraguirre, destroyed five years ago. Full of the joy of this hope, that same evening she wrote to her husband that she had met Louis Duville and agreed to go out with him. 'When he came in, my first movement was to run away, but he held me back and I realised at once that we were forgiven. My love, I am preparing a beautiful surprise for you.' She thought that Louis Duville would come to see her the next day; she was wrong, grew anxious, lost confidence and decided to remind him by a letter whose tone could not fail to touch him. She asked Mme Dajeu if Louis Duville still had his flat in the Quai Voltaire and, to excuse a question that might betray her, she added: 'I promised him an address that I had mislaid.'

'Better write to him at Valronce as he will be away until next Saturday. But, tell me about him and his parents. We like him, although we don't really know him. He is agreeable, isn't he? and not at all provincial for a seed merchant. You know, my husband is one of the biggest clients of their firm. How do they live, what are they like?'

Mme Zaraguirre appeared to search her memory, and while she spoke she relived her first visit to Valronce, her first walk

with Louis Duville, their happy engagement and the arrival of
M. Zaraguirre.

She wrote to Louis Duville at Paris. It was a daring gesture, but
she was prepared to be still more audacious in order to be able
to tell her husband that M. Duville had turned over the page on
which was written the circumstances of their quarrel. 'Soon we
will all be together again at Valronce,' she told herself. Unable
to dismiss this beautiful picture from her mind, she awaited the
end of the week, and neither the evening parties in Paris nor
the pleasures of fashion could make her forget that time was
passing and that she would go home wretched if Louis Duville
denied her the chance of achieving her sentimental ambitions.

They went out together the following Saturday. Louis Duville
took her to the park at Saint Cloud, whose long perspectives
seemed to have been traced by melancholy. Walkers were rare
in the November twilight, and even by the ponds there was
no one. Expecting to have tea at some elegant place, Mme
Zaraguirre was wearing little high-heeled shoes that were very
inconvenient for walking. Tottering, she clung to Louis Duville's
arm, and feigning fatigue, let herself be dragged along in the
manner of coquettish women, who, in order to attract, assume
the airs of a child. At first they did not refer to the past. Louis
Duville thanked her for her letter, she sighed, he seemed bored
and soon suggested that they should sit on a bench.

'Are you frozen?' he asked.

'Nearly.'

'Then let's go back.'

'Ah! no. I haven't the courage to leave you already.'

He looked at her. 'You haven't the courage to leave me. You?'

'Ah! don't speak of that! How could I, loving you, have done
what I did? Tell me again, I beg you, that you forgive me.'

'Tell me that you loved me,' he replied.

'Ah! yes, I loved you, yes, I loved you,' she said, and she gave
him her hands which he kissed.

They could not escape the past for long. Days at Valronce and in Lorraine emerged one by one from their conversation; they remembered the same moments with the same emotion and yet their thoughts were not alike: while Mme Zaraguirre, slightly committing herself, wished only to obtain from Louis Duville a favour that would add to her husband's happiness, Louis Duville, still moved by the memory of his beautiful love, hoped to avenge himself on a man who had humiliated him. When the comedy they were acting was over, Mme Zaraguirre thought that she had reconquered a heart free from bitterness and Louis thought that he had re-won a woman who loved easily. Besides, she attracted him. 'Let us go out together this evening,' he said.

'Ah!' she said, 'I feel I came to Paris only for you.'

He returned with her to the Dajeus' and invited them to the theatre; they accepted and throughout the evening Mme Zaraguirre shone with all the glitter of her marvellous plan. She was conscious that Louis Duville admired her, and, deciding to speak to him frankly, asked at what time they could meet the next day.

'At five.'

'And where will we go?'

'Where you like.'

'Very well, let's stay at home. It will be easier to talk there.'

Before going to bed Louis Duville reread Mme Zaraguirre's letter. So much goodwill made him uneasy, and the next day he felt guilty at going to see her.

'Come, come, I have something important to tell you, but I don't know how to put it. At one moment I dare and then I lose courage, I am embarrassed, help me. It is a long story,' she said, leading him to the little drawing-room.

'Then I shall have all the longer to enjoy hearing you talk. Your beautiful accent brings the past to life again . . .'

'Ah! the past, must we always return to it?'

He stood leaning against the door and she sat on a low seat by the chimney. 'According to my husband, women only use friendship to fill the time that they cannot devote to love. Apart from those moments, he says, when they take a purely personal form to give themselves up to the power of imagination, anybody will do as a companion. He says that friendship is a masculine feeling. You know him and . . .'

'I thought I knew him,' Louis Duville interrupted.

Mme Zaraguirre looked at him sadly. 'Irony makes frankness impossible,' she said, and, still quoting M. Zaraguirre, she went on: 'A shared love that makes a woman perfectly happy cannot satisfy a man on every level of his life. I am jealous of my husband's regrets. I want to end them.'

'Well?'

'Well, do you think that if your father and my husband met as we have by chance, yes, do you think that M. Duville would have treated him as you have me? Do you think that a reconciliation between them is possible?'

'I don't know, but perhaps slowly, very slowly . . .'

'Very slowly? Why? Why should your father resent us now that we are reconciled? Tell him that. It is through loyalty to you that he does not want to see us. There is no longer any misunderstanding between us. Is that true, yes or no? Well, talk to him.'

'One would have said that you were asking me the easiest thing in the world. You are very persuasive, but you haven't yet made me believe that your happiness depends on this little matter of friendship.'

'Little matter!' she cried.

'"Fidelity is faithful to feelings rather than to the being who inspires them. The loved one is only a support for these feelings, and love is a need that must have an object to test it, and thus prove itself between two infinities." Do you know who said that?"

'No.'

'Your husband.'

'Ah!' said Mme Zaraguirre, 'he was talking of love, I am talking of friendship.'

'And I of fidelity,' answered Louis Duville, and he added: '"Fidelity, the fine flower of surrender, is the only true sum of all efforts, all moralities, all resignations. When infidelity is absent the beautiful sirens desert us and go to sing elsewhere, believe me. Fidelity is royalty, it is taking a long risk and counting oneself for nothing." That is what your husband used to tell us.'

'He was not unfaithful, it was I who took him from you. I want to give him back. I am jealous of his nostalgia, and what is more how can I be happy as long as my conscience is not clear?'

'A clear conscience? I see you want every happiness. Be patient: stay here and wait.'

'Wait, when I am leaving next week?'

Listening to her, Louis Duville had found his means of revenge: 'Leave,' he said. 'Your presence here to some extent forces me to take a course that in your absence I would have no reason to follow. Can we discuss this again on your next visit?' She looked at him and came towards him.

'I trust you. You have a heart and you will help me, won't you?'

For answer, Louis Duville took her in his arms and held her there without a struggle. 'Give me a little of your time and I shall do all you want,' he whispered in her ear. She was certainly not in love with Louis Duville, but he did not repel her. She thought him in love with her, and in order to strengthen her hold over him she pretended to share the emotion that he apparently felt. 'It is madness, we are mad,' she murmured, then, quickly disengaging herself, she added: 'If I stay for you, will you stay for me?'

'I shall prolong my visit. What are you doing this evening?'

Mme Zaraguirre was bound that evening by an invitation that suddenly no longer tempted her: 'It is the season for colds,' she said, and went to find Mme Dajeu who was resting in her room. 'I am sorry, but I don't feel well. Look, I am shivering, I have a fever, and I would be in bed if Louis Duville did not insist on my drinking some soup with him.'

'Didn't I say that there would be some broken hearts?' replied Mme Dajeu. None the less, she disapproved of her breaking so late an engagement to a dinner given in her honour and advised her to overcome her fatigue and put in an appearance. Mme Zaraguirre coughed: 'No, I am too ill,' she declared.

This behaviour so displeased Mme Dajeu that she mentioned it to her husband in the car. 'She must be mad to dine at a restaurant when she is feeling ill,' she said.

'If Louis Duville makes love to Mme Zaraguirre, I would rather he did not do it in my house,' replied M. Dajeu.

* * *

An attraction and a temptation can often prevent lucidity. Although he was fascinated, Louis Duville was able to behave with skill during dinner: he spoke of the flight of time and condemned tyranny, and Tijo, as a result of certain comparisons, lost its charm in Mme Zaraguirre's eyes. She had a suspicion that for five years she had lived a life of penance;

she saw pleasure in an innocent light and even wondered if M. Zaraguirre's generosity had not been a manœuvre to keep her hidden from the admiration of others. 'He has always treated me like a child, a toy, a live doll,' she said, 'and while it is true that he has devoted himself to satisfying my wishes, he has certainly never been interested in my soul.'

She made this confession to a man who treated her not only as a pretty woman but also as an intelligent person whose every word deserved consideration. She confided in him, he listened and answered in such a way that she began to think that M. Zaraguirre, by affectionate and unconscious paternal egotism, had imprisoned her youth and stifled her personality.

'Ah! How right I was to love you,' he murmured.

'You have confused me,' she said, 'I no longer know who I am.'

'I will teach you who you are and what you deserve. I admire and pity you.'

Women like nothing so much as being pitied. To pity them is a duty of courtesy and the man who does not pity the woman

whom he strives to make happy ends by giving her nothing but reasons for pitying herself.

What Louis Duville said lacked the force of persuasion; Mme Zaraguirre could not in good faith have accused him of having influenced her, and yet he was able to make her admit that she was a victim and had rights.

'If you pity me, it is because you understand me,' she said.

Carried away by this new condition, she assumed languid airs, slower movements and desolate smiles.

After dinner they walked in the Bois de Bologne where the lake had kept the grey light of the day. They wandered along the shore, made several suitable remarks on the landscape, stopped, started again and strolled on until the moment when the silence, their solitude and the hour drew them slowly into each other's arms.

Amorous exchanges of which conscience cannot approve become in a sense heroic acts, and remorse may be said to increase the pleasure of kisses stolen from it by love. Mme Zaraguirre, overcome by a fairly ordinary passion, did not reason and try to control herself but gave herself up to it, took the side of her guilt and delighted in it. Louis Duville took her home with him and did not bring her back to the Dajeus' door until shortly before dawn. Two telegrams, which she slipped without opening under the cushions of the chaise-longue, were waiting for her in her room, and when she caught sight of the imprint of her lips on the glass that covered her husband's photograph she turned her head away and threw herself on her bed. M. Zaraguirre seemed to her then all the more worthy of respect because she had been unfaithful to him, and for the first time she realised what she owed him. In this way the deceived often assumes a sacred importance in the eyes of the deceiver. Asking herself questions, Mme Zaraguirre found herself excuses and soon fell asleep.

It was Mme Dajeu who woke her the following morning: 'It is late, I was worried at not having heard you. How do you feel?' she said.

'Wretched.'

'You should not have gone out last night. You were very foolish.'

'Foolish? Why?' answered Mme Zaraguirre.

'Answering one question by another is always a bad sign. He is charming, isn't he?'

'Do you think so?'

'Stop defending yourself! Louis Duville is in love with you, I know it and I envy you, for is there anything better than knowing oneself loved?'

Imprisoned in her remorse, Mme Zaraguirre weakened at these words; she felt her solitude and, moved by the wish to leave it, she cried: 'Ah! If you knew the truth, you would see how much I am to be pitied! The same two men, each in his turn, divide my heart and my conscience!'

'Two men? You?'

'Alas!' said Mme Zaraguirre, and without further preamble she told Mme Dajeu how she had been engaged to Louis Duville, how she had married M. Zaraguirre and how, the night before, she had let herself be led beyond the limits prescribed by flirtation.

Her frankness and the peculiarity of her case made their impression on Mme Dajeu, and the end of this confession started an enduring and intimate friendship between them.

'As you have been so frank, be completely so: are you in love?' asked Mme Dajeu.

'Men are strange, they are really fond of each other,' replied Mme Zaraguirre. 'My husband misses M. Duville's friendship, he misses Valronce, and that casts a shadow over our life together. I gave in to Louis Duville to get a favour from him, and then I lost my head, I forgot my motive and let myself go too far.'

'So much the better! Going too far makes duty less painful. A woman who loves her husband may deceive him to further his ambitions. For that matter, is it really a deception?'

It is neither love nor misconduct, it is rather lucidity that makes the deceiver's role an odious one. Once thought has intervened, the act is no more than the result of a calculation.

'What are you going to do now?' said Mme Dajeu.

'If I go away, and leave Louis Duville a second time, he will hate me for ever. And if I stay ...'

'Stay! He loves you, he wants to please you, and I am ready to swear that in a few days from now you will be able to write to M. Zaraguirre to join you at Valronce. Marriage has so many drawbacks, but at least it has the advantage of providing wives with honourable excuses: a woman deceives her husband because she loves him and it is because she loves him that, once she has reached her aim, she can break an attachment that would be guilty if it were disinterested.'

'Thank God, I am not disinterested,' said Mme Zaraguirre. 'Listen, darling, promise me to keep this a secret between ourselves.'

'A secret? You can be certain, I am silent as the grave,' replied Mme Dajeu.

The two ladies were there when Louis Duville was announced. He had told Mme Zaraguirre that the naked winter light emphasised the beauties of architecture and had promised to take her to lunch at Versailles.

They went by the Bois de Bologne, the banks of the Seine and the park at Saint-Cloud: 'Do you remember?' said Mme Zaraguirre as they crossed the park. No make-up masked her pallor, she lowered her eyes and her lids were pink. Louis Duville was calm and everything in their behaviour proved that their intimacy of the night before had drawn them farther apart instead of nearer together.

'"Certain memories have nothing to do with memory, but are suggested by the heart to the mind,"' answered Louis Duville. 'Do you know who said that?'

'Ah! You are trying to hurt me! Why do you tease me? I am worried. Advise me, should I leave or stay?'

He stopped: 'I think about you ceaselessly, I see you everywhere; look,' he said, showing her the trees, 'those branches, those twigs only draw against the sky today aspects of your face and being. You know that I love you, and yet you hesitate? Will you then never prefer me to all this?'

'Yes,' she said in a breath, and murmured: 'Love . . .'

He smiled at her. They went on their way and he spoke of the palace of Versailles and the silence that the exiles leave behind them in the houses and gardens from which they were expelled. 'It is a silence haunted by reproach, it is a silence of inconsolables and from generation to generation the curious feel uneasy in a room where the death bed still awaits the departed.' These remarks enforced meditation and Mme Zaraguirre, who would have liked to tell him of her conversation with Mme Dajeu, dared not do so and was silent. They visited the palace and, in the manner of lovers, went over the Trianons: 'Walking in Versailles is like walking in romance,' said Louis Duville.

'How well you explain things,' she said. 'Everything you say is so easy to understand. Where are you taking me tomorrow?'

'Tomorrow, alas, I have to return to Valronce.'

'To Valronce, already! Ah! if only you bring me back good news! I shall see no one while you are away. I shall shut myself up at the Dajeus'; they are discreet, aren't they?'

'I have no idea, but don't give them reasons for being discreet. Don't talk to them about us.'

Mme Zaraguirre now feared that she had been imprudent, and anxious to hear Mme Dajeu renew her vow of silence she said that she was very tired and had to go back: 'I must lie down before dinner,' she explained, 'or I shall not be able to keep upright tonight.'

M. Dajeu had lunched with his wife that day and had been inquiring after Mme Zaraguirre's health.

'She is better, yes, she is better, poor thing,' Mme Dajeu had replied.

'Poor thing? Why poor thing?'

Mme Dajeu had pretended not to hear. M. Dajeu had been surprised, he had insisted and she had merely shaken her head until, seeing that he would insist no more, she had revived his curiosity by making him suspect some secret: 'Ah! If you knew,' she said.

'If I knew what?'

Mme Dajeu was vain. Her vanity conquered her discretion and under the seal of secrecy she repeated to her husband what Mme Zaraguirre had told her: 'It is simple, she wants to end a quarrel that is making her unhappy. She loves her husband, poor thing, and how she must love him to deceive him! What a romance! What a story! If I read it in a book I would not believe it. And what do you think about it?'

In this way Mme Dajeu did Mme Zaraguirre a great wrong.

'I think this is a disgraceful story from beginning to end,' M. Dajeu had declared. 'Your "How she must love him to deceive him!" does not excuse, in my opinion, the misconduct of a woman entrusted to us by her husband. In such a case as this, to protect her is to encourage her. You can say a relation is coming to stay, you can invent any excuse you like, but I insist that Mme Zaraguirre ends her visit under another roof than ours.'

'Impossible!' Mme Dajeu had exclaimed.

'Impossible? Would you rather that I spoke to her?'

'No.'

'Well?'

'Well, you are making a martyr of me,' she answered, and she had cursed her husband's severity until Mme Zaraguirre had come in from her walk: 'Here you are, at last. It is such a bore, such bad luck, but something too tiresome for words has happened,' she told her. 'An uncle of my husband's is coming to Paris to see a doctor. He always stays here and I have no other room to give him but yours.'

Mme Zaraguirre's politeness made Mme Dajeu's task easy.

'Please don't apologise. When is your uncle arriving?'

'Tomorrow. If I were alone I would send him to the devil, but I am married and that spoils everything. Promise me not to be angry with me.'

'And you must promise me not to breathe a word to anyone of what I told you this morning.'

'Whom would I tell it to?' answered Mme Dajeu.

Unexpected inconvenience can sometimes produce a feeling of shame and loneliness, and although Mme Zaraguirre understood Mme Dajeu's reasons she nonetheless felt abashed and humiliated at having to pack her bags in a hurry and move to a hotel.

She spent the evening with Louis Duville. He tried to console her: 'You need have no regrets, the Dajeus' atmosphere does not suit you. You are my secret, we will live in hiding,' he told her, and Mme Zaraguirre, sad, exiled, and believing herself loved, saw herself as a romantic heroine and found comfort in being unhappy.

The next day, she moved to the hotel. Mme Dajeu helped her. She had reserved for her a charming suite, filled with flowers sent by Louis Duville and M. Dajeu. The bedroom was grey and the drawing-room was hung with red damask framed in gilt mouldings. Mme Zaraguirre liked it, but her first move was to run to the window and lean her forehead and her hands against it. The garden of the Tuileries, bared by winter, was spread out beneath her. 'How austere it is, I miss my birds and the shade of the foliage at Tijo,' she said.

'You miss the past, the present and the future, you want to be at Tijo, at Valronce and in Louis Duville's arms all at the same time,' answered Mme Dajeu.

Mme Zaraguirre covered her ears with her hands, turned round quickly and cried: 'Ah! Don't talk like that, I beg you!'

'Very well, let's talk of something else. What dress will you wear this evening?'

'This evening? I am not going out,' said Mme Zaraguirre, and as soon as Mme Dajeu had left her she wrote to M. Zaraguirre: 'I shall be tortured by remorse if I have delayed in vain the moment of seeing you again. Louis Duville is going away for a fortnight. He has advised me to wait and promised, when he said goodbye, that before long we shall be crossing the threshold of Valronce. That is well worth a sacrifice. I think only of you, my love, I am sad, I am alone, I long to embrace you. What will Christmas be without you, without your kisses, without hearing you tell me "You smell blue"? I am yours and nothing else.' Mme Zaraguirre was sincere. She was weary, afraid and full of remorse, and, wishing to forget, what better means of distraction could she find than to dress and join Mme Dajeu at midnight at a Spanish ball, where she was much admired.

At Valronce, Louis Duville often thought about her. Nevertheless, he did not mention the cause he was supposed to plead, and although he tried hard to appear natural his parents noticed that he was absent-minded, that his conversation was less free than usual and that he seemed preoccupied. Mme Duville trembled: 'I am sure he has bad news for us,' she told her husband. 'He has probably been driven to regularise a young man's escapade.'

'What do you mean by that?'

'An illegitimate child, boy or girl, and the result: a forced marriage.'

'What an idea,' answered M. Duville. 'Love, even when it is happy, is an anxiety that disturbs peace of mind, and possibly Louis has fallen in love with a young girl, a flower who intimidates him.'

'If it's to do with a flower, he would not mind telling us about it,' replied Mme Duville. 'Try to question him.'

M. Duville refrained from doing so and felt himself the more justified when his son's good humour soon returned.

Nothing had changed at Valronce in five years: once a week, the colonel danced there with young people; M. and Mme Duville had the same friends, the same occupations and the same desire to see their son satisfactorily married. In the mornings the two MM. Duville left Valronce together for their office, and these days M. Duville was surprised to see his son stop on the way to post a letter himself. These letters addressed to Mme Zaraguirre contained neither lies nor deceptive declarations, but kisses, expressions of impatience and reminders of shared memories.

* * *

The Airmail Company conveyed the post by aeroplane from Paris to Dakar, and from there by fast despatch-boats to the principal ports on the Atlantic coast of South America. When he reached the end of his journey, M. Zaraguirre found news from his wife. While he was touched by her good intentions and did not object to her meeting with Louis Duville, he was displeased that she had accepted to go out with him alone and was even more so when he learned, a little later, that she had moved to a hotel and had delayed the date of her return. He wrote to her begging her to come back: 'Don't humble yourself, don't beg at the Duville's door, I don't like it. What effect do you think your presence could have on Louis' decision? If he is sincere, we will know it, and it will be on my arm that you cross the threshold of Valronce.' He also gave her the name of the steamer on which he wished her to embark.

Mme Zaraguirre read this letter to Mme Dajeu. 'I shall be alone at sea at Christmas, among strangers! Ah, how badly I have calculated; I thought I would gain everything by giving way but instead I have made everything worse. Louis Duville loves me and wants to keep me here.'

'That was to be expected. As for me, I now think that you ought to go.'

'That would mean a final break between Valronce and us. How can I explain that to my husband?'

'You will explain nothing and he will think that Louis Duville has not kept his word. Better a break between Valronce and you than a break in your marriage.'

'You are right. I shall go.'

'And now I must leave you,' went on Mme Dajeu. 'You are expecting Louis, aren't you? Goodbye, darling,' she said, and went away.

Mme Zaraguirre's clouded eyes, and the tears on her cheeks reflecting the lamp-light, halted Louis Duville when he arrived. 'How beautiful you are, like hoar-frost,' he said.

'No, I am frozen,' she answered, giving him the letter that she had received from her husband.

Seeing M. Zaraguirre's handwriting again, Louis Duville saw him and heard his voice in imagination. Jealous, distracted by old memories, he remained pensive, and Mme Zaraguirre, who was no longer crying and was sitting by the fire, looked up at him as she had done, years ago, during her first lunch at Valronce. Louis Duville, meeting her glance, found his lost fiancée once more: 'Ah! you, you,' he said.

'Yes, us. I hate these moments when the present seems to be slipping away and I would like to die.'

'To die so as to plunge into the past, to go back to the time before there were any consequences?'

'Yes, exactly, I don't want to live because living means leaving you.'

'Leaving me? No. I shall go with you. We shall make the journey together and your husband will be told that he can return to Valronce if that can console him for having lost you. He made no secret of taking you from me, and I shall not hide the fact from him that you are no longer his.'

Mme Zaraguirre complained loudly and begged, 'No, no, I will kill myself sooner than allow that.' This reaction increased Louis Duville's rancour, strengthening his desire to prolong M. Zaraguirre's waiting and to deprive him of the woman he had lost to him. 'And aren't you yourself wounding him each time you look at me?' he asked.

Terrified by the idea of Louis Duville following her to South America and talking to her husband, Mme Zaraguirre found herself in the position of a gambler who, having lost everything, sells familiar objects in the hope of buying them back the next day. To gain time for escape, she involved herself further and confessed that she was torn between love and duty.

'What duty, other than letting yourself be tyrannised by a man who has kept you under his authority for five years and refuses you the innocent pleasure of staying a few more days in France? Believe me, you have the right to a little liberty.'

'It is true that I am much to be pitied,' said Mme Zaraguirre, and she started to cry again.

Louis Duville took her in his arms and dried her tears. Tenderness and sadness each produce a similar effect of languishment, and there was so much melancholy in the kisses with which she responded to his that he thought them tender when really they were sad. 'Come,' he said, 'we will go from Mediterranean beaches to the snows of the Tyrol.'

'The Tyrol must be so beautiful! The Dajeus mean to spend Christmas and the New Year there.'

'Come, leave Paris tomorrow. Let us live together for three weeks of a life that I long to spend entirely with you. Give me that proof of love, calm my jealousy, heal my bitterness and allow me to believe in you.'

Mme Zaraguirre thought that by staying longer she could keep at bay the dangers threatening her marriage and safely withdraw from a situation that she had considered desperate.

On the evening of the following day, the 21st of December, after confiding in Mme Dajeu, she left for the South of France, very ashamed at going with her lover to the shores where her husband's love had twice brought her.

Eight days later M. Zaraguirre received a letter from his wife which thoroughly displeased him. 'My beloved, our wishes are the same: we want to be together again. You know that it is for your sake that I deprive myself of you, and yet you scold me? Your letter made me miserable. If I leave tomorrow, I shall not arrive home till the 3rd of January. You haven't thought of that, and knowing that you would be sad to think of me alone, at sea, for Christmas and the New Year, I have accepted to spend them in the Tyrol with the Dajeus. They are delighted to show me a country which they describe as full of mountains and marvels. We must leave this evening. How can I tell them, at the last minute, that you are forcing me to go home and punishing me as if I deserved it? As it is too late for us to end or begin the year together, let me at least see the mountains, the forests of fir and the snow; that will console me. Don't refuse me this pleasure. I shall be back in Paris on the 16th of January, in exactly three weeks, and on the 21st I shall embark on the *Alcantara*. The crossing will seem endless until I reach you. I don't know yet where I shall be living in Austria.

The Dajeus mean to go from towns to villages and from hotels to inns. I shall be lost in the snows! We shall live like mountaineers! Don't you see? Write to me in Paris. Your letters will be forwarded. I love you, I adore you, don't scold me, my love. I shall come soon, yes, very soon, wait for me, etc.' M. Zaraguirre called his secretary: 'My wife and I are rivals in impatience and surprise. She is sailing on the *Alcantara* on the 21st and complains at having to make the long journey alone. So I shall go to meet her and we will come back together.' He sent for the list of boats leaving for Europe and booked a passage on a steamer bound for Genoa which would call *en route* at Villefranche on the 16th of January.

* * *

Whether it is evident or disguised by seasonal moods, fine weather haunts, even in winter, the Mediterranean coast. The air one breathes there defies convention, encouraging those who have come for relaxation to take liberties and to find excuses for them. Louis Duville and Mme Zaraguirre lived stolen hours. Away from home, they believed themselves unrecognisable; they were imprudent, let themselves be seen too much, and on the night of the 31st of December had supper, alone together, in the big dining-room of a casino. It was a gay and brilliant

gathering, there was dancing and paper streamers and pellets of cotton-wool were thrown from table to table. Louis Duville and Mme Zaraguirre, a little apart from this revelry, exchanged sighing looks and smiled gravely, as lovers do who share a secret and think of the night to come.

At midnight the lights were put out. The cymbalist in the orchestra played the twelve strokes of the hour, and when the chandeliers were relit Louis Duville and Mme Zaraguirre were standing hand in hand. Then, before sitting down, she threw a handful of streamers at random into the room; one did not unroll and, falling on a distant table, upset the glass of a man who, quick to retaliate, rose and turned round. This middle-aged man was having supper with some business people, big merchants and bankers; his wife was sitting opposite him and he called to her: 'Look behind me, far back, in the corner on the left, isn't that Louis Duville with his ex-fiancée, or am I getting short-sighted?' This couple, who lived near Valronce, knew the Duvilles quite well and had been present at the party given on the eve of their son's projected wedding. Most of the people at their table knew Louis Duville and some of them had met Mme Zaraguirre in Paris with the Dajeus.

'Mme Zaraguirre, Louis Duville's ex-fiancée? How is that?' somebody asked. On which the neighbours of Valronce took deep breaths and told everything they knew of the story. This made a great stir. The presence of Louis Duville and Mme Zaraguirre, alone together in this place, gave their intrigue an official character and became first the subject of bold conjectures, and then of false assertions which rapidly found their way to Valronce.

Two weeks later, M. Duville was leaving his office when a neighbour, just returned from Nice, stopped him to praise the beauties of the South of France.

'We saw your son on New Year's Eve. He seemed to be enjoying himself.'

'I'm glad to hear it. Was she pretty?' asked M. Duville.

'Pretty? Prettier than ever. Younger than she was five years ago. Very elegant and very *décolletée,* but as she was in black my wife thought she must be a widow. A widow! If Zaraguirre were dead, we'd know it. What a story! They talked of nothing else at our table. There was even a question of marriage. You have certainly been secretive at Valronce, but our society is too small to keep something like that hidden for long.'

'And what then?' said M. Duville.

'You want me to say what I think?'

'Yes. Usually I don't care about public opinion, but in this case I confess that it interests me.'

'Don't worry. Zaraguirre is admired; who doesn't admire him? But nobody nowadays would go so far as to pity him. All's well that ends well. What a story, my dear fellow, what a romance!'

'And what indiscretion,' answered M. Duville in the tone of somebody who finds himself, despite his prudence, dispossessed of a secret.

However cautious he might be, M. Duville had no reason to doubt the word of an honest man, who was certainly not lying when he described having seen Louis Duville and Mme Zaraguirre proclaim their intimacy and behave like lovers. Having spent his days in the country, between his place of business, botanical excursions and the Herbarium, he was not surprised to find himself ignorant of one of those situations which, in certain circles, add spice to the pleasures of conversation, but he was shocked by it. Conscious of the humiliation that M. Zaraguirre was undergoing, he condemned the man responsible for it and wondered whether a desire for vengeance, even more than another feeling, had not governed his son's behaviour. This suspicion horrified him; he tried to discard it but could not, and the friendship he still felt for M. Zaraguirre prompted him to ask him back to Valronce and welcome him with open arms. Their quarrel no longer had a reason. That day, returning home, he avoided the Herbarium and went straight to the library where the colonel was reading *The Conscript of* 1813 aloud to Mme Duville. 'I am suffering from stupor and consternation,' he told them, and after repeating what he had just learned he pleaded, in all sincerity, M. Zaraguirre's cause: "'Your son must not marry a woman who no longer loves him enough. She has left Valronce and is going away with me.' That's what he told me in the past. And now Louis is living with her openly. The injury he is doing Zaraguirre is utterly hateful to me, and Zaraguirre must know that it is. When he was happy at Louis' expense we could only refuse to see him. Now the roles are reversed."

'It's a bit much!' exclaimed Mme Duville. 'Which of the two was the first to take her away from the other? Tell me. I am asking you. Each in turn, if you please. I hope you're not going to start feeling sorry for Zaraguirre. It is only what he deserves. Louis has finally paid him back in his own coin? Well, so much the worse! He has taken back what he was owed. So now they are equal, and not a moment too soon. That's how I see it, it's nothing very serious.'

'And what would you say if he was forced to marry her?'

'He marry that woman? She marry him? Never! If she had loved Louis she wouldn't have even looked at Zaraguirre and ...'

'Wait a moment, be fair,' interrupted the colonel; 'Zaraguirre didn't stop himself from looking at her.'

'And why should he have stopped himself? Men have the right to look at women. In my opinion, that is what they are there for,' replied Mme Duville, and just as she had been defending her son against M. Zaraguirre, she now took up M. Zaraguirre's defence to attack the unfaithful wife: 'A she-devil, a man-hunter, who was only put in the world to do mischief. Poor Zaraguirre! Poor Louis!'

'It isn't always others who deceive us, it is sometimes our own hearts,' M. Duville remarked.

'I pity people who are reduced to dreaming of the past,' went on his wife, and, returning to the time of the engagement, she betrayed her bitterness, her sadness and her disappointment: 'When it was all over I felt so stupid at having been so trusting and happy and having invited so many people to witness our discomfiture. Yes, what a she-devil; there are enough men in the world, why did she have to choose just those two, one after the other?'

'And why did those two men have to choose her? There are other women, if I'm not mistaken,' declared the colonel. 'I see no end to this business. Will Zaraguirre get a divorce? What will Louis do? What will you do? So many questions which only the future can answer. Meanwhile, I would rather be at my house than yours.'

He took his watch from its fob and made it strike without looking at the dial. 'Seven o'clock, the hour for heroes, it is time for me to go; goodbye, dear friends,' he said and he went away.

Mme Duville thought of her son's future and the more she thought of it the more she longed for Mme Zaraguirre's downfall. 'You'll see, she'll hang heavy on his hands,' she said to her husband. 'He knows it, he daren't confess it to us and that's why he has been behaving so oddly just lately. Didn't I guess that he had bad news for us? Is it my fault that I guessed rightly? You, needless to say, thought he was in love with a flower. A pretty flower, I must say. Oh! it's too easy being a botanist, you live in the clouds, your feet are off the ground, you are above reality. But I'm not an ostrich, I look facts in the face and I should be less frightened if Zaraguirre were less proud. Do you remember what he used to say? "The really deceived man is the one who knows it and accepts it. He thinks he is still a man when he is no more than a screen. A piece of furniture." Can you see him being a screen?'

'No.'

'Neither can I and it's that that's worrying me. If I were you, this is what I'd write to him: "I was angry with you for taking away Louis' fiancée but now I forgive you on condition that you don't give her back to him." It's obvious.'

'As obvious as a dagger thrust,' answered M. Duville. 'He will realise that, without considering his dignity, we think him ready to accept an odious bargain merely for the pleasure of seeing us again; he will despise us and shrug his shoulders at our idiocy and we shall have added to his loneliness. No. Let us show him what we really feel. Of course he knows we are incapable of rejoicing at his defeat and also incapable of indulgence towards Louis, and yet I am afraid that our silence would have something equivocal about it. Isn't it unlikely, in fact, that we should know nothing about a state of affairs that Louis has seen fit to advertise for such a long time that people are even talking of marriage? From my side of the partition that circumstances have placed between us I have remained Zaraguirre's friend, and Louis' conduct obliges me to tell him so.'

M. Duville sat at his writing-table and his wife, leaning over his shoulder, watched his pen trace these words: 'Come quickly, we are expecting you.'

M. Zaraguirre's secretary received this telegram in South America, and immediately forwarded it to him.

It was evening, the voyage was nearly over, the steamer was at sea off the coast of France and M. Zaraguirre was walking on deck hand in hand with two young women, when M. Duville's message reached him. He was annoyed: 'We can't lunch in Nice tomorrow, as I promised, nor can we dine on the Paris train.' The young women whom he addressed sighed, their eyes filled with melancholy and with one voice they answered: 'What a pity!'

'You are so pretty that we shall meet again,' went on M. Zaraguirre; then, to be polite, he explained, laughing: 'My wife was to arrive in Paris in the evening and I intended to join her there tomorrow, but she preferred to stop in the country with some friends who live between Paris and the coast. So I shall join her there instead.'

He was very irritated that Mme Zaraguirre, ignoring his advice and his orders, had once again delayed her departure. 'It will be on my arm that you cross the threshold of Valronce,' he had written to her. He found her insistence vulgar and her obstinacy in bad taste, and even his conviction that she had asked M. Duville to telegraph him in her place, to increase the pleasant surprise she had prepared for him, did not make him indulgent or alter his bad humour. He was inclined to see what displeased him as ridiculous and his position displeased him greatly. The idea of finding his wife with Louis Duville and of being welcomed by her to the house where he had first seen her was disagreeable and governed his reasoning. In his turn determined to surprise, he did not reply to M. Duville and the next day left Villefranche in a hired car. After raising his hat repeatedly to the pretty women who were waving their handkerchiefs on the quay, he set off for Valronce where he was due to arrive in the late afternoon.

Night falls early in January. Carried along the main roads in his little mobile cabin scented by mimosa and violets bought at Nice, M. Zaraguirre, after dark, let his thoughts drift to the beasts of the forest, to streams, to the sound of footsteps on the earth, to the mystery of movement and to many things forgotten in sunlight. The nearer he got to Valronce the more he tried to distinguish features of the countryside, and soon, going through villages, he recognised the porch of a church, a café, a tobacco shop.

Mme Duville was in the linen-room where, helped by a housemaid, she was sewing ribbons on cloths and shawls for a charity sale, and M. Duville was working in the Herbarium, when M. Zaraguirre arrived. Faneau heard the noise, ran to the door and on to the front steps, then, seeing M. Zaraguirre, backed into the hall. M. Zaraguirre slowly climbed the steps. 'It's only me,' he said, 'and I am happy to see you again.'

'Happy? And what about me? I thought I was dreaming,' answered Faneau. 'Madame is in, she is upstairs,' and with a gesture inviting M. Zaraguirre to follow him, he showed him the staircase.

'No, tell her that a traveller has returned. Be mysterious and discreet.'

A single lamp was burning in the library. M. Zaraguirre turned away from it and waited standing in the shadow. Suddenly, he felt a deep emotion: the thought that his wife was near, that scarcely one minute separated her from him, that surprise would make her waver between laughter and tears and that he would hold her in his arms, conquered his severity and bad temper. He now saw only love and clumsiness in the wrongs he had blamed her for; he regretted having criticised her, accused himself of injustice and adored her again. Impatient, he started towards her when a noise stopped him. Excitement made him close his eyes and when he opened them it was to see Mme Duville throw herself on his neck and to hear her cry: 'You, you! It is too wonderful. It is like a miracle. How have you come so far in so little time?'

M. Zaraguirre looked at the open doorway. He thought that his wife, informed by Faneau, had decided to play once more a favourite trick; that she was in the hall and was approaching on tiptoe to appear suddenly and surprise him as she had done so often at Tijo. He believed her to be a few steps away and it was for her ears that he answered in a voice whose teasing tone she would recognise: 'I got your telegram yesterday at sea off Villefranche. I had sailed without warning my wife. Why should I have warned her? She has abandoned me for nearly two months! Two months. Ah! the unfaithful creature, I wish she could hear me now and that my anger would make her tremble.'

'Two months, two months, don't,' begged Mme Duville. 'We knew nothing about it, no, nothing, I swear. It was only the day before yesterday that we heard about it, and from a neighbour who saw them on New Year's Eve at Nice. That is the reason for our silence. They are both equally guilty, I grant you, but while Louis is a man and a bachelor, she is a woman and married, as you know better than I.'

M. Zaraguirre put his hand on her arm: 'I am not curious,' he said, and he asked where M. Duville was.

'He? At this hour? He's at the Herbarium. Where did you expect him to be? He is being told you are here. Come, come, let's sit down'; and in a hurry to go back to what interested her, she went on: 'You aren't curious because you know everything. For me, it's different, and there's a detail in this business that intrigues me: were you with them when they met again?'

'No.'

'She was in Paris?'

'Yes.'

'Why?'

'Because I had sent her there.'

'I don't understand it at all: you complain that she abandoned you and yet it was you who decided to separate? Still, it's all to the good, as in that case Louis is less to blame. You will admit that wives nowadays really ought to stay faithful. Love is no excuse these days; it is no longer a pastime, not even a distraction. They have the telephone, the cinema, the wireless, cars and the marvellous progress made in aviation; all that ought to be enough to keep them happy: but oh dear no, they still want men as well.'

M. Zaraguirre smiled and said that he would go out to meet M. Duville.

'In this cold? How eccentric! You, at least, haven't changed. All the same, cold seems to be the fashion: Louis sent us a postcard from the Tyrol. Such a beautiful country, it's sickening. But, go, go, I won't detain you; there will be plenty of time tomorrow to have a serious talk.'

M. Zaraguirre threw his overcoat over his shoulders and went out. Once outside, he clenched his fists, struck his chest and stayed on the steps to breathe the air of this deceptive night. It was there that M. Duville found him.

'I am happy,' said M. Zaraguirre.

'You can only be so out of goodness,' answered M. Duville; on which, reviving a boyhood custom, they leant side by side against the front of the house.

'To be forsaken is bitter for someone who knows the sweetness of forsaking. How surprising loneliness is! I will not talk of it again,' M. Zaraguirre said at last. 'As we are not philosophers, we have feelings inside us that nothing can civilise. We can guess each other's thoughts, so why speak of my departure and my return, and of the five years that have gone by? We must not forget, but we must be silent.'

'That will be the surest way of hiding nothing from each other,' answered M. Duville.

Mme Duville called them, threatened them with pneumonia and announced that dinner was ready. She had changed into a dress the colour of Parma violets; M. Zaraguirre complimented her on it, she cooed and during the meal the conversation was limited to agriculture, animals and the weather.

At the moment when dinner at Valronce was ending, Louis Duville and Mme Zaraguirre were preparing for a farewell evening. They had been in Paris since the morning. Mme Zaraguirre, who had only been kept with Louis Duville for three weeks by fear, was about to escape from the trap into which she had fallen and Louis Duville was as unwilling to hold her back as he was tired of a revenge which he now saw to be base. He had soon pitied Mme Zaraguirre for the confidence she had shown in him; he was ashamed of misleading her and it was as much to avoid giving himself away to her as to redeem himself in his own eyes that he had promised, before the end of their journey, to call M. Zaraguirre back to Valronce. This false proof of love eased his conscience. If a little poetry still clung to the memory of their first transports, it was because they had concealed from each other the motives that had inspired them.

Mme Zaraguirre and Mme Dajeu had met neither in the South of France nor in the Tyrol. The one had much to tell and the other wanted to hear everything; they had seen each other again that afternoon: 'My husband is angry with me,' said Mme Zaraguirre. 'I have had only one letter from him dated a fortnight ago, and what a letter! He writes that if I don't decide to return, he will decide to come and fetch me. And what if he has left? If he comes in while we are talking? What a dream! I would take his hand and tell him, "Come, we are going to Valronce."'

'Be serious and tell me more about Louis Duville. Is he still mad about you?'

'He loves me and still thinks that I love him. What a miracle! But I have had enough of this acting, I confess. It's tiring, you know. I am dining with him tonight and in five hours from now I shall be at Cherbourg. Ah! how impatiently I am longing for the 21st! Do you understand?'

Mme Dajeu understood.

As for Louis Duville, he was in such a hurry to tell his father that time had dissipated his grudge against the Zaraguirres that he regretted having asked Mme Zaraguirre to dinner, out of politeness. He set out to fetch her without enthusiasm and was waiting for her at the gate of the lift when suddenly she fell from the sky in a golden cage accompanied by the sigh of a vertical breath of air. Through the arabesques of this cage he watched her put on her gloves and, when the door opened, she took two paces forward and said: 'Here I am.' The fulfilment of her wish, the knowledge of her near departure and the end of a bad dream had restored to her the expression and the movements that M. Zaraguirre preferred, and Louis Duville found himself face to face with a stranger who had the look and the scent of a bouquet of a thousand flowers. Nothing about her was addressed to him; he felt it and was interested in her.

* * *

The one truly hopeless state is that of regret. Fickle, with something childish about her, Mme Zaraguirre had become once again her husband's creation. If Louis Duville had never seen her like this it was because, since their meeting in Paris, she had tried to please him, and also because he had only considered her as the object of his revenge.

'Where would you like to go?' he said, and she chose a restaurant where there was dancing.

Just as a widower, who falls in love with a wife whose value has been revealed to him by her death, longs to bring her to life to cherish her and ask her forgiveness, so Louis Duville longed to lead Mme Zaraguirre back to the present. It was in vain. She had escaped and the distance now separating them could not be surmounted by a single love. He reminded her of Saint-Cloud, Versailles and their travels. While he talked she nodded her head as if to the sound of pleasant music, and though she did not disown the past there was a kind of denial in the way she spoke of it in her turn, as of a time which duty obliged her to renounce.

'I don't know what blinded me, what prevented me from even imagining you as you are today,' he told her.

'It is love that blinds. One sees better from far away.'

'Are you trying to tell me that you are far away from me?'

She protested: 'No! I have no wish to be unkind to you, don't let's spoil this last evening.'

'You are a temptation to which I was wrong to yield, a dream I was wrong to dream.'

Mme Zaraguirre lowered her eyes and murmured: 'Don't misunderstand: I want to be reasonable but I shall never forget you. I shall miss you a great deal and shall go to Valronce only to see you again.'

'You will come back soon? You won't change your mind?'

'No,' she answered, smiling at the thought that from now on it would be she who would do Louis Duville a favour by going to Valronce.

A man and a woman who have not been real lovers and are not real friends do not find much to say to each other. Louis Duville asked Mme Zaraguirre to dance, she accepted and soon wanted to go home. He took her back. They said goodbye at the door of her hotel; Mme Zaraguirre repeated several times: 'I hate goodbyes, they are too sad,' and hastily disappeared.

Louis Duville passed the rest of the night drinking with pretty women; he went to bed in the morning, woke in the late afternoon, sent flowers to Mme Zaraguirre and set off without having seen her again.

No one was expecting him at Valronce, where Mme Duville was entertaining a small party of about twenty people in honour of M. Zaraguirre. She had hoped that with the aid of a crackling fire, young laughter and the smell of lavender floating through the house, he would recover the gay mood of past evenings there. She had welcomed her guests with her customary turbulence, but animation had soon flagged and the colonel, to avoid a threat of silence caused by curiosity, had declared that winter did not suit the roads: 'The upper road is nothing but a hole, a real battle-field. It reminded me that in 1917 . . .' Exclamations interrupted him and M. Zaraguirre came in, imposing, at his ease, his eyes large and his forehead lightly touched by the breath of adventure. The women ran to him, he pressed them each in turn to his heart, held out both hands to the men, was introduced to the young people, and seemed so lively, so happy at being liked that M. and Mme Duville decided that he had already banished from his thoughts the being who had banished herself from his life.

M. Zaraguirre was incapable of disappointing. His readiness to be amused, his understanding of other people's feelings, filled the young men and girls with wonder. The whispering and the bright eyes of the girls attracted him more than did the men, who wanted to profit from his experience and tried to detain him. 'Experience does not come with age, but from the nature of human beings. Its only value is as an element of comparison,' he told them after dinner, and then went up to the women. Each of them had loved him more or less secretly, and Mme Zaraguirre's absence did not displease them. Overcome by the romantic languor which his presence produced, they felt their hearts turn into galloping horses, carrying off their thoughts like young ladies to a lovers' tryst in a real forest.

Knowing how much his mother enjoyed entertaining, Louis Duville was not surprised to find the house illuminated at midnight. He heard music and gently pushed the drawing-room door ajar to see who was inside. Facing the company and leaning against the piano, a child was singing accompanied by Mme Duville. Something gothic in her bearing attracted attention, and it attracted Louis Duville's. When she stopped singing someone rose to compliment her, and this someone was a tall man whom Louis Duville recognised. He shut the door and went up to his room. When the time came for goodbyes, his father was the only one to notice a green felt hat on one of the chairs in the hall. He accompanied M. Zaraguirre to his room, waited until Mme Duville was in bed and went in to see his son. Motionless and apart, they looked at each other.

'Zaraguirre is here? Since when and why?' asked Louis Duville.

'Bad news travels fast,' answered his father.

'What news?'

'Don't play the innocent. He left for Europe without even troubling to tell his wife.'

'Is that my fault?'

'Yes.'

Then M. Duville told him everything that he had heard, describing M. Zaraguirre's arrival and quoting his first words: 'To be forsaken is bitter for someone who knows the sweetness of forsaking.' Louis Duville understood how reason and feeling had prompted his father to recall M. Zaraguirre to Valronce, and yet he was furious: 'You have both been too ready to believe a lot of gossip. Zaraguirre? I shall go straight to his room and swear that his wife and I are only good friends.'

'That is what every unfaithful man or woman swears to the person they have deceived, it is what a well brought up man tells everybody and it is also what Zaraguirre has let many an anxious husband believe. You wanted your revenge? That he could understand, but his wife has no excuse; she has simply been inconstant. It is not so wrong, and yet it is worse. Where is she?'

'In Paris. He knows it and he knows she is sailing . . .'

'He knows it and has not gone to join her? Why? Why, when he received an invitation that might well have been addressed to them both, did he not first fetch his wife? Believe me, he knows all about you, and he also knows that I have only shown him friendship because of your misconduct.'

'Our misconduct? You have profited by it. His wife . . .'

'Enough! And when is she sailing?'

'On the 21st, on board the *Alcantara*.'

'Very well, let her go!'

'And am I to let her go without warning her of what she will find? No. I shall prevent her from being taken unawares. I shall help her to find excuses; it's the least I can do, surely?'

'Yes, it's the least you can do. Warn her and make her go. Take her on board, if necessary.'

'Listen,' said Louis Duville slowly, 'couldn't you help me? What advantage is there for you in that marriage breaking up? Tomorrow evening, when you come in, couldn't you pretend to have met someone who contradicted everything you believed to be true? Your conscience would be troubled, you would talk to Zaraguirre and tell him: "I wonder if we haven't judged too hastily? Perhaps we were wrong; the world is so mischievous. It seems that this story was invented by spite. Apparently they were not staying at the same hotels at Nice and in the Tyrol. I am worried." Like you, Zaraguirre would be afraid he had been unjust, and then what would he do? A doubt makes an explanation necessary. He would hurry to send for his wife. I wouldn't arrive till later, and we should all be together again at Valronce at last. That is your dearest wish.'

M. Duville agreed.

'And if he is slow to be convinced, if he doesn't send for her before the 21st, you will nonetheless have planted a doubt in his mind from which they will both benefit if they don't meet again till they reach Tijo!'

'You have feeling, you are right, and I shall talk to him tomorrow evening at the Herbarium. As for you, keep quiet about what you mean to do. Don't give that woman any hope that might keep her here. If Zaraguirre doesn't hesitate she will hear from him, but if he hesitates and she is still in Paris he will be suspicious of her reasons for staying.'

A human being may be distracted from the evil he has done, but cannot be consoled for it. Louis Duville left at once for Paris and arrived at Mme Zaraguirre's about midday. Her little drawing-room was filled with luggage, still open, from which rose the sweet scent of dresses and linen already laid out in large trunks. As she was half-dressed, she slipped on a dressing-gown and came in smoking a cigarette, with bare feet and untidy hair.

She smiled but her expression grew slowly graver: 'You're not at Valronce? Where have you come from, Louis? Are you ill?' she said. 'The light seems to be blinding you. I am so fond of the blue January sky.'

'The light hurts me today.'

To cheer him up she tried to joke, drew the curtains, lit the lamps and said: 'Now it is night time. What more do you want?'

'Darling, listen, I have come from Valronce.'

'You have? Why? What is the matter?'

'Your husband . . .'

'Ah! Don't! I should have guessed from your manner that you had bad news. What about my husband? Is he ill? Is he . . .'

'He is at Valronce,' answered Louis Duville.

'At Valronce? He, at Valronce? Why? What has happened?'

'He has been told about us.'

'Told about us? And what then?'

'Well, he has been told the truth.'

'What truth?'

'The truth about us.'

'No, no, that's impossible, I won't have it, no, I can't bear it. And who has told him the truth?'

'Gossip.'

'And what brought him back to your house?'

'Friendship.'

'And you have seen him?'

Louis Duville told her in what circumstances he had glimpsed M. Zaraguirre at midnight in the drawing-room at Valronce.

'Ah!' she exclaimed, 'he was listening to a young girl singing! He rose to compliment her!'

'No, it was not a young girl, it was a child of thirteen or fourteen.'

'Ah! How attractive her innocence must have seemed to him after all the evil he has heard about me! What am I to do? How can I make him understand . . .?'

Louis Duville advised her to return to Tijo.

'Return to Tijo as if nothing had happened? And risk his throwing me out of the house? Make myself a laughing-stock? No, never. I shall go away, yes, but I shall go to Valronce and I shall explain, I shall defend myself, I shall fight. What proof has he against me, after all?'

'But how could you know that he is at Valronce?'

'From you.'

'And how could I know?'

'From your father.'

'And my father, who shares your husband's convictions, would have asked me to tell you?'

'No, but we are good enough friends for you to have done so. My husband knows perfectly well that we are reconciled.'

'If we were only that, he would not be at Valronce.'

Mme Zaraguirre ran to the window and drew back the curtains. The blue January sky, the movement in the street, the sight of so much that was indifferent to her fate, drove her back into the room: 'Ah!' she cried out in anger, 'they have lost no time in believing appearances and finding a pretext for meeting again. And so I must be sacrificed to their old friendship? No, no, I shall destroy it. Yes, I shall destroy their friendship. Your father has accused me, my husband has condemned me, and you are ready to accept it? But I shall not accept it.'

'You would be at Valronce if your husband wanted it.'

'How can he want it when his suspicions are confirmed by your father's attitude? Ah! how mad I was to love you. It is all your fault and you don't say a word in my defence.'

'It is in your defence that I tell you to leave.'

'Leave? And play my enemies' game? Leave him alone for one more day among people who can only harm me? No. It is in my interest to forestall what he may yet be told. So they don't want me at Valronce? That makes no difference to me. My husband is my husband and I know him better than you do. In an hour or two he will get a telegram from me. I bet you that he will come tonight and I shall tell him the truth at once.'

'What truth?'

'The truth about us.'

'I don't understand.'

'Why don't you understand? It's simple enough. I shall say to him: "I know there has been talk about Louis Duville and me. It was inevitable, and as I love you I haven't even listened to these lies. But you have. It is finished, all over, I shall never forgive you. Is it my fault that a woman can't be seen twice with a man without malicious people assuming the worst? What if we were seen together in the South of France and the Tyrol? Where is the harm? The same people meet at the same places at the same time of year. That is life. Think about it, to be unfaithful one has to be secretive. And, tell me, have I made a secret of anything?"'

'You are talking like Mme Dajeu.'

'So much the better, she has good sense. You are like your father and think of nothing but how to get rid of me.'

'What you say is unfair and unkind, but it can't be helped. The only thing that matters to me is that you don't act against your own interest. Believe me, don't telegraph your husband.'

'I repeat that I understand him and know what I am doing. It is my life at stake, not yours.'

'My love . . .' he began.

'Ah! That is easy to say. Leave me alone, I beg you.'

'And let you do something stupid? No,' he said, and while he paused, at a loss for arguments, Mme Zaraguirre, convinced by his silence that she had won, wrote to her husband: 'Come, I love you, let us go home together. Telegraph hour of arrival by car or train.' She rang for the chambermaid and gave her the paper, saying, 'It's urgent'; then she added, 'It is time I got dressed.'

'What have you written?' asked Louis Duville.

'That's my business,' she replied, and he left her.

* * *

M. Zaraguirre was not touched by the telegram he received from his wife. He tore it up and threw it in the fire: 'Who told her I was at Valronce?' he said to M. Duville. 'And if she is innocent, why doesn't she come to me herself?' If M. Zaraguirre had often loved other men's wives, he refused to be one of those husbands whose wives belong to other men. He did not hesitate, and answered at once in these terms: 'I am so afraid of being lonely in your company that I prefer to go home by myself.'

Part Three

After Louis Duville had gone, Mme Zaraguirre imagined the answers she would give to the questions her husband would be sure to ask her, making of them a delightful dialogue at the end of which M. Zaraguirre would have to admit that he had been wrong. From time to time, to give more authority to one or other of the replies she intended to make, she struck the top of her dressing-table a sharp blow with her comb.

Mme Zaraguirre had religious convictions which the gravity of her situation forbade her to neglect and, judging that the moment had come to make a sacrifice which would attract divine protection, she ordered a car and went to Chartres. 'The blue of the stained-glass windows in the cathedral is pure blue,' M. Zaraguirre had told her. 'In it one feels the will of someone creating the colour.' The grandeur and mystery of this magnificent place reduced the sense of her own importance to nothing. At first this pained her, then she resigned herself to the idea with such modesty that she was rewarded: 'How can I, who am of so little account, have great faults and commit great sins?' she thought. She wandered in the twilight and sacred cool, calling on God for help: 'I am a soul in distress. My God, let Your eyes be not too big to see me.' Nevertheless, her brain was so full of plans that she could neither collect her thoughts nor pray single-mindedly. She lit candles before the dark Virgin, knelt at her feet with lowered head and promised lavish alms to Saint Anthony of Padua if he would help her recover, not peace for her conscience, but her lost tranquillity of mind.

Night had fallen when she started her return journey. The feeling of having lost control of her destiny, which she had placed in the hands of God, made her idle and absent-minded and increased her loneliness. Wanting to see a bright fire, to confide in someone and to hear human speech, she decided to stop at Mme Dajeu's.

She found her having tea alone with her husband who was reading the newspaper: 'Murders, nothing but murders,' he was saying when Mme Zaraguirre came in. 'I hope I'm not disturbing you,' she said. M. Dajeu kissed her hand, folded his paper and left.

'You disturbing me? Never, darling,' said Mme Dajeu. 'But where on earth have you been? You look as if you had come from another world.'

'I made a pilgrimage to Chartres.'

'A pilgrimage, how silly, leave that to unhappy people!'

'Yesterday I could still decide my own fate but from today God will decide it for me.'

'God? Why Him?'

'Because I asked Him.'

'It's not possible!' exclaimed Mme Dajeu. 'Do you think that was quite wise?'

'The future will tell,' Mme Zaraguirre answered gravely.

'Another secret? Tell me, you're not sad? What can I do for you? Champagne?'

'Perhaps,' answered Mme Zaraguirre.

'Very well, you shall have champagne.'

'Just a drop because I am in a hurry to get back; yes, I am in a hurry and at the same time I am afraid.'

Mme Dajeu sent for the wine; two lamps were turned out, thus providing a frame for their confidences. They lighted cigarettes, Mme Zaraguirre talked and Mme Dajeu waited until she had finished her story before exclaiming: 'It is perfect! You have got what you wanted: your husband is back at Valronce. It is now half-past five; according to your calculations he should arrive between eight and ten and you have everything ready to prove your innocence! What more could you wish for? You'll come out of it all right, I assure you, and I understand less and less why you went to Chartres.'

'My husband says that praying is thanking in advance.'

'An artistic thought! Don't let's wander from the point, we must get back to reality. First: a reasonable man is satisfied by his wife's lies; second: be firm, be proud and reproach him: "I am tired of being judged unfairly. If you think that I enjoyed myself in Paris you are wrong. I only stayed on for your sake. Yes, I sacrificed myself for you. And all that time you were accusing me of Heaven knows what wickedness. Louis Duville would no more think of making love to me than of entering a convent. I swear it and he would tell you so himself if you asked him. Oh, it's too unfair! Do I look like a woman who could lie to you? Tell me. You know me, don't you? I love you, I admire you, I think only of your happiness and only believe in our life together. Did I ever complain during the five years at Tijo? Tijo! Dear Tijo! Where I spent the most beautiful years of my life. Ah! If I had only known, etc."'

Mme Zaraguirre clapped her hands: 'It is word for word what I was meaning to say to him! How did you guess?'

'Experience, intuition, habit, call it what you like,' answered Mme Dajeu. 'Have you kept the car?'

'Yes.'

'You are impatient, that's natural; let's go to your hotel and stay together till dinner. You want to make yourself beautiful for him, don't you?'

When she reached the hotel Mme Zaraguirre asked the porter if there was a message for her.

'Yes, it came just now,' he answered, and he handed her a telegram on a little tray. She took it and pressed it to her heart.

'Come,' she said to Mme Dajeu; 'let's go up, I don't want to read this here.' And she added in the lift: 'I knew he would answer me, I was sure I was right.'

She ran to her little drawing-room, opened the telegram, uttered a cry, staggered and collapsed.

Mme Dajeu thought she was dead, killed by too much happiness. She informed the servants, sent for Louis Duville, summoned a doctor and returned to the little drawing-room while Mme Zaraguirre was moved to her bed. She picked up the murderous message, read it and placed it, as she would have a revolver, in the drawer of Mme Zaraguirre's small bedside table.

Mme Zaraguirre was not dead, but she had lost her life. Her fainting was followed by a nervous attack and then by a state of prostration interrupted sometimes by outbursts of anger and sometimes by sobs. Mme Dajeu saw in it the proof of a perfect feminine education. None the less, as these changes of mood were rather alarming, she strove to remedy them either by encouraging rebellion when Mme Zaraguirre wept or by approving when she did rebel, and, more often, by giving her sedatives. This régime suited Mme Zaraguirre. She soon felt better and, after three days, recovered her spirits and looked at herself in the glass. However, she talked of suicide: 'To die, to die, to go away. Ah! There is no place for me down here.' Mme Dajeu then hid the sedatives and deplored the absence of Louis Duville who, recalled by his father, had gone that morning from Paris to Valronce, which M. Zaraguirre had left the previous day.

M. and Mme Duville welcomed their son as if they knew nothing of the difficulties in which, by his own fault, he had been involved. They treated him with the discretion on which the mutual understanding of this family had always depended, and Louis Duville was grateful. His mother thought he looked ill and told him so, to which he replied that he was indeed tired and that on his next holiday he would avoid big hotels and live like a hermit.

One evening, while he was helping his father to put the Herbarium in order, he interrupted his work and talked about Mme Zaraguirre. He had made up his mind to devote himself to her and, although the situation in which he accused himself of having placed her made her less glamorous in his eyes, he was ready, if need be, to marry her. 'I cannot leave her on her own,' he said to M. Duville.

'Leave her on her own, after having broken up her marriage? At least wait for her to leave you before you think about leaving her. Follow Zaraguirre's example. Couldn't you have prevented her from writing to him and thus proving that she had heard from one of us that he was here? I no longer look on that woman as Zaraguirre's wife and I refuse to meddle in an affair that can have no more consequences as far as we are concerned than any of your other adventures. Can we leave it at that?'

No coolness between them resulted from this conversation. Mme Duville observed the vow of silence imposed by her husband; life at Valronce recovered its familiar rhythm and Louis Duville, happy to be kept busy by the work which his long holiday had made him neglect, stayed over a fortnight before returning to Paris. Like any man of feeling in whom circumstances have weakened desire, he wished Mme Zaraguirre every possible happiness, but a happiness that kept her away from him. Only a great love could contemplate without alarm the complications in which he had involved her, and if certain memories still moved him he was now able to rationalise his devotion.

Mme Zaraguirre, for her part, thought only of her husband. Eager to plead her own cause, she had written him countless letters which she had been prudent enough to reread and then to destroy. Thus, as the snow of January fell on the window-panes, so paper flakes, the snow of uncertainty, fell from Mme Zaraguirre's hands in the little drawing-room of a hotel in Paris. She had no talent; the right note and convincing arguments were beyond the powers of her pen; she saw that by explaining she compromised herself and that her lies became more and more dangerous the further she perfected them: 'My letters lack the taste of tears! Ah! What am I to do? Now I only have you,' she said to Mme Dajeu.

'Come, come, you can count on Louis Duville as well.'

'Don't speak to me of him. He has caused my misery! He should have forced me to leave, he should have bound me and carried me on board. Yes, everything is his fault, absolutely everything.'

'That is why you can count on him. As to your misery, your husband's severity is to blame for that. If M. Zaraguirre had been indulgent, your crime would have been the same but he would have forgiven it.'

'Severe or not, how do you expect me to say to him: "I am too generous, it was for your sake, darling, that I gave in to Louis Duville"? Ah! Louis was sincere and I wasn't; he loved me, that's what ruined everything.'

'Don't reproach him for having loved you when you encouraged him.'

'What else could I have done? Ah! I don't want to hear any more about love. I have your friendship and that is enough.'

Mme Dajeu, who was already wondering what she would do with Mme Zaraguirre if she continued to lean only on her, and who knew, besides, that M. Dajeu would object to the constant presence in his house of a woman whom he considered in a false position, was extremely embarrassed to hear her repeat: 'Yes, your friendship is enough,' and extremely relieved when she added, pensively: 'And everyone will say that I have been deserted by my husband and Louis Duville at the same time. There is no limit to spitefulness.'

'Alas, poor darling, you know that only too well. People are capable of making out that Louis has run away for fear that you will hang round his neck.'

'Me? Hang round his neck? Could they say that? But that's terrible.'

'Yes, it would be terrible, and that's why I advise you not to reject him. Stay on friendly terms with him, and show yourselves about together if only for the sake of appearances.'

'Appearances! He certainly owes me that after all the harm he has done me.'

'He is attractive to women; they would soon take him away from you; and then, you need him.'

'I do?'

'Yes, because I don't see who else could keep you informed of your husband's plans and intentions. M. Duville will certainly know them; Louis will have questioned him and can report to you everything he hears at Valronce. Who knows? Perhaps M. Zaraguirre only wishes to give you a lesson.'

Mme Zaraguirre was still living in the hope which the last part of this interview had planted in her mind when she received a parcel from South America containing all the photographs that M. Zaraguirre had of her at Tijo. A few lines were enclosed: 'Madame, by order of M. Zaraguirre, at present in London, we are having all your personal possessions and all your books sent to you in Paris. We are making the necessary arrangements with regard to your bank account, which will be supplied with funds. We remain, Madame, . . . etc.' Mme Zaraguirre wept alone and, ashamed of this excess of misfortune, she did not even mention it to Mme Dajeu and awaited the return of Louis Duville.

He found her lying on a chaise-longue in a dark corner, which the bright lamplight made by contrast increasingly obscure. Wearing a pleated coat of grey muslin, she was no longer either a flower or a fruit but a stone effigy, carved on a memorial tomb. She looked at him, grew gradually livelier, gave him her hands to kiss and offered him tea: 'The taste of tea is so pleasant, especially in winter,' she said. 'Before the 1914 war my parents were *en poste* at Saint Petersburg and I spent two Christmases with them there. Ah! I should have stayed there; the Russian soul, that is what I need!'

'The Russian soul?' he said, laughing. 'What an idea! You are always unpredictable, always unexpected.'

'Unexpected, that is the word. Nobody expects me any more. What should I do? Where can I go? Ah! I am angry with you! Why didn't you make me go back to Tijo?'

He answered that in his opinion it was not too late for her to go back and that this brave gesture would be certain to touch M. Zaraguirre.

At these words she sat up and cried out: 'Good advice, indeed! Look at that! Read that! And tell me if I can make a brave gesture. Look at it, read it,' she repeated and, angrily snatching the photographs and letter from a small table, she scattered them round the room: 'It's finished! It's the end! He has even sent away the memory of me! How cruel, how unfair! You alone could have prevented this.'

Louis Duville read the secretary's letter and felt resentment towards M. Zaraguirre.

* * *

Memories of a period that still continues belong to the present and lengthen its duration. Mme Zaraguirre became aware of this. By putting a ban on their life together, her husband had deprived their past of a future, and Mme Zaraguirre, looking behind her, saw their years of marriage break away from the continent of their life to form an island on which she would never again set foot. It is then that thought becomes a ghost, wandering in those places to which destiny has denied admittance; and while this ghost goes from the house to the promenade, from the door to kisses once trustingly cherished, arrows of memory pierce a living heart.

Yet Mme Zaraguirre's vexation exceeded her sorrow; her pride defeated her love, fury took the place of dismay and she considered M. Zaraguirre unworthy of being loved. It was not him that she missed, but the walls, the garden, the cluster of tree-fern in the middle of the drawing-room, the spacious life that she had enjoyed and everything over which she had reigned at Tijo. This royal condition had raised her above reality and it was for her lost kingdom that she wept. Mme Dajeu blamed M. Zaraguirre and supported his deserted wife. She sang her praises and helped her to imagine the pleasant future to which her youth entitled her. Louis Duville pitied her. She was not fickle, the evils of infidelity urged her to prudence and rather than seek possible conquests she preferred to return to her former lover. Louis Duville could not evade this decision, which bound him all the closer to Mme Zaraguirre as he recognised his duties towards her.

Mme Zaraguirre knew that love is more easily betrayed than confidence and it was her confidence in him that he dared not deceive. She was able to show him that her happiness now depended only on him, and, jealous of the Duvilles, their house and the life he led there with them, she gave way to excessive sighing each time he left her to return to Valronce.

In his absence, and always accompanied by Mme Dajeu, she visited a large number of flats to let. She had very decided ideas and several months passed before she found what she wanted. She finally took a flat on the edge of the Bois de Boulogne, on the ground floor of a house next door to Mme Dajeu's. A small garden was attached to it. As it was too late in the year to start work that the summer would have interrupted, she camped among the plaster, ordered potted plants and concentrated on the garden. 'I am in a hurry to settle in. I shall make it wonderful, yes, wonderful. Ah! I wish the summer were already

over. The summer is like a long yawn,' she said to Mme Dajeu in the easy tone that she unconsciously assumed when quoting M. Zaraguirre. On Saturday and Sunday evenings she put on a white lawn dress and blue satin pumps and, holding a black paper fan or a shawl, she waited for Louis Duville at the threshold of her garden. Then he let himself be carried away by the grace of this woman who was M. Zaraguirre's invention, and in the garden full of flowers and the empty house spent passionate hours when seduction and desire resolved themselves in surrender.

In July Mme Zaraguirre had to go to Lorraine where an accident to her father kept her for some time. She had led her parents to believe that the climate at Tijo, too exhausting for any length of time, had forced her to settle in Paris; they supposed that her husband deplored it as much as she did and that their marriage was flourishing. 'Luckily I have good friends,' she told them, 'and you will be surprised to hear that Louis Duville is one of them. Ah! How funny life is! He even seems to want to make love to me. Him? Make love to me? How ridiculous!'

A woman who has been left once is always afraid that she will be left again and that is why Mme Zaraguirre, forgetting that meetings can be as dangerous in the country as in a city, forgetting in fact her own history, had insisted that Louis Duville should not go to Paris while she could not be there herself. 'At Valronce there is nobody with whom you are not familiar; it is the reverse in Paris, where novelty lays its snares at every turn.' Since his liaison deprived him of the pleasure of casual love affairs with the women he called 'momentary beauties', Louis Duville preferred Valronce to Paris. There he rested from Mme Zaraguirre's constancy and suspicions, and the young provincial girls whom he had scorned now seemed to him more charming and mysterious than fashionable women. The advantages of freedom prevented him from missing Mme Zaraguirre and he dreamed of never seeing her again. Slavery had emboldened his imagination; he was attracted by everything that had once bored him, he liked simplicity, was interested in the beautiful young girls whom his mother invited in the hope that one of them would take him in hand, and soon became the hero of the parties at Valronce. The colonel asked him to spend the evening of the14th of July at Dentelle; he accepted, arrived last, found the drawing-rooms deserted and heard a distant voice. All the other guests were in the garden and formed a circle round the piano, which had been moved beneath trees decorated by fairy lights. Louis Duville approached quietly and recognised the young singer whom he had glimpsed at Valronce six months before. When she had finished her song she curtseyed, smiled, spun round and disappeared into the shade of the garden with the other children. He learnt that she was thirteen years old, that her name was Léopoldine, that she was the youngest sister of one of his army friends, and that M. Zaraguirre admired her.

* * *

When Mme Zaraguirre said goodbye to her parents she let them understand that she was going to rejoin her husband. The year had reached the beginning of September; Mme Duville was taking a cure at a watering-place; M. Duville was abroad collecting plants and Louis Duville took Mme Zaraguirre to a sunny beach.

During the summer exclusive colonies are formed, governed by pleasure. Siestas, colours, highly-scented flowers and activity stimulated by some quality of the climate – all are reminiscent of ancient Turkey. Nothing is impossible; the trees are near to the sea and music comes from rooms where glances make assignations. All this improved Mme Zaraguirre to a wonderful degree. The beach, laziness and a life without shocks suited her, and she received more than one love-letter by moonlight. She responded by loosening her hair which hung to her waist. The wind disturbed it, veiling and unveiling her face, lifted it, lowered it, and moulded it round the white tower of her body. Women rose at dawn to go and spit on her footprints in the sand. This new aspect appealed to Louis Duville, and although he hoped she would fall in love with another man, as soon as someone looked at her he wanted to keep her. Proud and annoyed to be her favourite, he gloried in this beautiful mistress and resented the fate that had forced her on him. He returned to Valronce dreaming of having a liaison with her that would not bind him.

The weather was fine under the roof at Valronce. M. Duville was pleased with the success of his botanical expedition; Mme Duville, refreshed by her cure, compared watering-places to open air drawing-rooms: 'That is the place to go if you want to see glory with the naked eye,' she told the colonel. He dryly advised her to measure her words: 'Glory is for soldiers, civilians only have celebrity. On one side a sword, on the other an umbrella.'

'What good is a sword when it rains? An ornament! I like what is practical, and I prefer an umbrella to shelter me.'

'To defend is to shelter,' roared the colonel. 'If we hadn't a sword, you wouldn't have an umbrella.'

'No sword, no umbrella? You make me laugh.'

The colonel rose: 'One cannot fight against ingratitude. Goodbye. The only true defeats are those in which the ideal has been wounded; the others are retreats while the ideal re-arms.'

Louis Duville and his father, who had been following this dialogue with amusement, rose in their turn and detained the colonel. The conversation changed its tone and they talked of the October flowers which are graver than those of spring and are plucked in a different spirit.

'Soon it will be October! Time rushes past,' said the colonel. 'Will Zaraguirre come back as he promised and is he still thinking of adopting Léopoldine?'

'He is in Europe and we expect him from day to day,' answered M. Duville. 'As for his plans concerning Léopoldine, I know nothing about them. If he adopts her, I shall be as pleased for her sake as for his. She would make Zaraguirre the happiest of grandfathers . . .'

'And he would make her a *prima donna*,' declared the colonel.

Then Mme Duville gave a sad description of the child's life: 'Her brothers and sisters have married and left the neighbourhood; her father hasn't a brain in his head, her mother only opens her mouth to complain, they haven't a penny to their name and their house is falling in ruins.'

'And would Léopoldine's parents agree to her leaving them? Would they let her go to live at Tijo, so far away?' asked Louis Duville.

'Her parents let her leave them? What a relief for them and what luck for her,' replied Mme Duville. 'Léopoldine is just fourteen. She is gifted, artistic and very intelligent. I'm sure she is quite capable of seeing things sensibly, and she is very fond of Zaraguirre. He will bring her back to France every year, she will travel, he will turn her into an accomplished young lady and, with such a dowry as he will give her, she will not lack for suitors. What a dream! It is like a story from the *Arabian Nights*. It remains to be seen whether or not it will come true. Zaraguirre has only mentioned it to me casually, he just said: "That is a child I would willingly adopt." Perhaps he has changed his mind. I am curious to know if Léopoldine suspects anything.'

Léopoldine came to Valronce the following Sunday and Louis Duville was there. She was not one of those children with the manners of a grown woman. She was unpretentious and unself-conscious and she envied nobody. She loved and admired her parents and lived happily in their dilapidated house, which was surrounded by large trees sheltering ferns. Her friends would call her by whistling beneath her balcony and she would leave and return to her room, vast and almost unfurnished, through the window. She would dance and sing in front of the mirrors leaning against the walls, and as she danced she would eat a

piece of cheese, a turnip or some fruit at the end of a knife. Dark, with eyes wide apart, she resembled a cross between a fairy and a hare. If no coquetry, no anxiety to please had yet entered her mind it was because she had always been loved, and pleased naturally, without knowing it. It was a fatal gift which women were beginning to criticise. Jealousy is caused by circumstances; appearance is among the most important of these, and certainly Léopoldine's suggested poetry. She had an eloquent pallor, a hand that held a secret and lips half-opened, caressed by the breath of her soul.

Louis Duville was very interested in this girl who had attracted M. Zaraguirre's attention, and curiosity had kept him at Valronce that Sunday. He was on the steps when she arrived on the arm of one of her cousins. He went forward to greet her and she gave him her hand, which was pretty but too long; he held it for an instant in his, without pressing it.

'Here you are at last,' he said. 'I do not know you, but I have heard you sing.'

'Oh! Sing!' she said.

'Yes, and it gave me so much pleasure.'

Embarrassed, she turned to her cousin: 'Come on,' she said, and they went into the house.

Our feelings influence us, revealing themselves in our countenance and regulating our movements, while our thoughts are unaware of them. Léopoldine had never been in love. Now her condition was altered and as she was completely inexperienced her friends noticed it. By tea-time, she had lost her laugh and her assurance, and the gaze she fixed on Louis Duville betrayed a great, sad timidity. She saw him three-quarter face; he smiled as he peeled pears for other girls and this made her suffer. How could she, a poor and simple girl without a smart dress or a fashionable *coiffure,* attract the attention of a handsome man of thirty-five, rich, elegant, heedless and accustomed to the admiration of women? Love had already exiled her from childhood, familiar landscapes and friends. No longer would she eat bread sitting on the highest branches of a tree; no longer would she jump from her window or dance in front of the mirrors, no, she would walk down narrow paths kicking a pebble before her. 'There is nothing for me now but to go fishing; I am alone, alone,' she thought.

After tea, Louis Duville went up to her and asked after her brothers.

'My brothers? They are really magicians. They play cards, they pour Chinese ink in their wine to discover what black tastes like, they make money by terrifying people and their wives eat nothing so that they can get into anything. Into anything, isn't that strange?'

'Yes, it is strange, but tell me, are you going to sing?'

'Sing? Now? Oh, no, it is late and I mustn't keep the friends who are taking me home.'

As he was about to insist, everybody rose to leave and he only had time to ask her if she would come back soon.

'Mme Duville has promised to ask me when M. Zaraguirre arrives, and I believe he is arriving soon. Will you be here?'

'Perhaps,' he said, and she went away.

M. Zaraguirre was expected at Valronce the following day.

'I am going to see to our business in the North,' Louis Duville told his father and, jealous, he left Valronce a few minutes before M. Zaraguirre was due to arrive. His mind was full of dreams and his heart was in nothing that he did.

In Paris he called on Mme Zaraguirre who, with Mme Dajeu, was giving precise orders to painters and upholsterers. 'Go away, turn round, close your eyes, don't spy on my secrets,' she called out gaily when she saw him come in, and before he had taken two steps she pushed him back into the hall.

'I am only passing through Paris, I have things to do in the North, and I came . . .'

'To ask me to go with you?' she asked anxiously.

There are people whom one only invites when certain they cannot accept: 'You wouldn't dare refuse me,' he said. She exclaimed: 'Darling, I am preparing our life together and you want me to leave all this work that I alone can supervise? Am I working for myself? No, for you, for us both. And besides, what would I do in the North? It's not that you are selfish, my love, but you can be inconsiderate.'

As the sky was blue and the weather mild, they went to sit in the little garden. Louis Duville listened to the gossip of the two ladies; he was bored and Mme Zaraguirre thought he was sad.

'You are very busy, I mustn't keep you, goodbye, dear ladies, and pity me,' he said, as he took his leave of them.

The two friends, left alone, looked at each other in silence:

'You see, I have spoiled him,' Mme Zaraguirre explained. 'He is used to my giving in to his slightest whim. I have no desire to bore myself waiting for him in hotel rooms. There are limits to kindness but none to the selfishness of men. I am moving in and I enjoy it, he ought to understand.'

'Prudence demands sacrifices from a woman for the man she cares for, especially if he is not her husband,' answered Mme Dajeu.

'Sacrifices? You are very kind! You forget that I have sacrificed everything for him.'

'Remember, darling, love only gives temporary guarantees. Before anything else you must conquer a man's conscience and his pity. If that doesn't prevent him from deceiving you it at least creates strong enough obstacles to make him think it over, and, more often than not, it prevents him from leaving you. Then honour is saved and that is the main thing. Believe me; you win if you lose nothing.'

* * *

The autumn colours in the country through which Louis Duville passed carried his thoughts back to Valronce, and in imagination he saw Léopoldine and her graceful bearing again. Would she be at Valronce that evening and would M. Zaraguirre talk of adopting her? Would she resist the temptation to be the cherished child of the best of grandfathers? No, she would not resist and her parents themselves would encourage her to accept so convenient an offer: 'Alas,' he thought, 'she is too young for me.' He envied M. Zaraguirre's ability to interest himself in her without offending convention, and his own age, of which he was innocent, seemed to him the worst and most unforgivable of sins. The restrictions that Mme Zaraguirre placed on his liberty added to his discomfort. There she was, and by her presence, her rights and her claims, she erected a wall in front of him that barred him from the future. Unhappy people are desperate to remould a past from whose consequences they suffer. He imagined what his present would have been if he had not wanted his revenge on M. Zaraguirre. The love he felt, that today seemed impossible, could have been considered in another light; and Mme Zaraguirre, who by his own fault was living in Paris, his for ever, this beautiful and rather touching woman whom at present he liked but did not love, would have been with her husband in South America.

While these thoughts filled his mind and troubled his heart, Léopoldine was making herself a wreath of heather, that austere flower, to wear to a dance at Valronce where she hoped to meet him again. Languor had increased her beauty and the reflection of love, the first reflection of her beautiful love, gave her that brilliance which springs from a tender feeling. Certainly, she was not yet a woman, but her manner promised much and that could not escape M. Zaraguirre's notice. He complimented her on it: 'You have grown up since January,' he said.

'Yes, I grew up in a day,' she said, then she added eagerly: 'Isn't Louis Duville here? Where is he? He told me: perhaps. Perhaps . . . There is some hope in that.'

'Where is he? I haven't the least idea,' answered M. Zaraguirre.

She danced. Everybody danced, but one cannot wait and be present at the same time. When one waits one is with the absent person, and Léopoldine was not there. M. Zaraguirre admired her; she knew that he was her friend and taking him by the arm she led him into the park, where they strolled under the limes that were yellow in daytime, but whitened by moonlight. 'In the evening I am often tired through having laughed or run too much. Tonight, I am nearly dead. Everything about me is waiting, my ears, my eyes, my arms. It is exhausting.'

'Your eyes, ears and arms are in your heart,' said M. Zaraguirre.

'I have given up waiting and yet I am waiting still. I am weak, I am mad. I am a weak, mad animal. My father's watch is out of order. It keeps its own time. That time is as true as the time told by the clock on the town hall, and yet it is despised. Nobody goes by it. My heart is out of order. People pay no more attention to its beating than they do to the time on my father's watch.'

'There are some cases when speech is superfluous. Besides, more often than not speech is merely an effect with no consistency, a slightly despicable organic reality which only achieves dignity when used by a martyr to free himself from the creative tyrannies bound to his nature. Everybody talks but few people say anything. Desire, on the contrary, is always worthy of interest. It sets the will in motion and the will guides desire to its goal. Desire, that is the key.'

'I want to be chosen,' murmured Léopoldine.

'Chosen? What an ambition!'

'And how can he choose someone he cannot see?'

'He cannot see you?'

'No. He is too far away and I can never catch up with his age. One night a friend of mine went to the theatre and suddenly fell in love with the leading actor. She borrowed money and went back to the theatre twenty nights running to watch him secretly. As for him, he never saw her. She waited for him at the stage door and clapped when he passed, and once he smiled at her. But he lived in another world and never stopped to say: 'Come and have supper with me, will you?' She broke her heart over that love. Now she is going to be married. It is the same with me. Louis Duville is on the stage and I am among the audience. A whole life without violets and lilies of the valley, think of it, a whole life. The bouquet one really wants is held by the hand one wants. Isn't that true?'

Old memories awoke in M. Zaraguirre: 'People, studies, pursuits, duties, all are futile if the heart does not lend them its colours and its movements. Don't think of age: when one loves, age does not exist.'

'And hope? What do you think about that?'

'About hope? I hope for it,' he replied.

* * *

Mme Zaraguirre's flat caused a sensation in Paris. The walls of the hall and dining-room were covered by white earthenware tiles with blue designs and in the drawing-rooms, which were whitewashed in lime, rows of candles in silver sticks lit Dutch pictures and mirrors in thick ebony frames. The windows were hung with double curtains of white muslin and pale blue watered silk. Rose-laurels, lemon-trees and climbing plants, entwined round bamboo poles, grew in silver tubs placed in the corners of the rooms. In the middle of the drawing-room a circular sofa, upholstered in plush with an Oriental pattern, surrounded a cluster of tree-fern reminiscent of the famous garden of Montserrat, at Cintra near Lisbon.

Mme Zaraguirre had scarcely moved in before her memories returned to her. From then on, as much through a desire for respectability as to prove to Louis Duville that she was not afraid to evoke the past, she spoke more and more frequently of M. Zaraguirre. She thought that she was not speaking of him but of an ideal man to whom she gave all the qualities that she denied her husband. In idle conversation, slowly, casually

and always without emphasis, she painted so fine a portrait of him that women fell in love with this ideal husband to a degree that made her jealous. She loved him, she clung to him, he was her creation and listening to her Louis Duville was the only one to wonder at the precision of her memory and to recognise M. Zaraguirre in this man whom she thought she had invented.

Mme Dajeu's world had become her own. She had friends in it and her love affair with Louis Duville had assumed a conjugal tone that no longer aroused any criticism. Docile, with reserve in her coquetry, she lived only for him. Instead of scolding him when he stayed away too long, she asked him questions about his business and his health then described the plays she had seen, the dinner-parties she had given and the dresses she had ordered. 'What shall we do next week? Where shall we go next summer? To the sea? I don't care,' she would say, 'as long as we are together.' And he felt her determination to belong to him. She was perfect and irreproachable, and if he was irritated by the reasons she gave him to respect her, he cursed his power over her and the obligations that this power created. She clung to him.

When they played cards in the evening at her flat and the candle flames trembled, she had a way of drawing on or slipping off a shawl that made the men run to the doors and windows, to open or to shut them. Everyone, even M. Dajeu, envied Louis Duville the devotion of so attractive, original and faithful a woman, and everyone, without knowing for certain whether she felt chilly or warm, protected her alike from draughts and gusts of hot air. They tried to please her and she thrived on it. When the clink of ice in the glasses disturbed the silence she would blink, bend back her head and say to Louis Duville: 'Sleighs in the Tyrol, do you remember?' Her words and gestures, the decoration and the lighting in her house, made a charming spectacle to which he was susceptible, but just as a leaf fluttering in the wind can distract notice from the finest scenery, so a vision fluttering in last autumn's breeze removed his attention from reality.

He had not seen Léopoldine since that Sunday in October when he had spoken to her for the first time. She had been at Valronce again, however, and if, on these occasions, he had shut himself up in the Herbarium or lingered at his office, it was because he had decided to avoid a meeting too distressing to his dreams. Troubled by a sense of the ridiculous, he had fled from Léopoldine, and she, at first disappointed by his absence and then humiliated by his indifference, came less and less often to Valronce. 'She must have some love affair in her mind, some cousin doing his military service who has forbidden her to enjoy herself while he is following the colours,' said the colonel.

'That is very likely,' answered Mme Duville; and nobody worried about her until the day when the colonel received an unexpected visit. 'While, with his back to the sun, he was reading a book by Georges d'Esparbès, his orderly came to tell him that a young girl had arrived: 'On horseback,' he specified. The colonel buttoned up his white cloth jacket and went out.

The young girl who wanted to see him was that friend of Léopoldine who had suffered so much for love of an actor. With a romantic appearance and a romantic soul, she had experienced despair at eighteen and it was natural that Léopoldine should have chosen her as confidante. The colonel helped her to dismount. 'Biscuits, syrup and strawberries. Close the blinds,' he shouted, 'it is stifling.' The drawing-room was streaked with light and shade; it became cooler and the girl in riding clothes sat on a sofa beneath a panoply. When the colonel had taken his place opposite her, on the other side of the table between them, she took an envelope from the bodice of her dress and handed it to him, saying: 'Look.' The colonel read the words: 'My country'.

'Our country, France?' he said.

'No, Léopoldine's; she wants to die.'

The colonel smiled approvingly: 'To die for one's country is the finest destiny,' he said.

'Her country is the tomb. She has discovered its charms too soon. She loves Louis Duville, he loves Mme Zaraguirre; she did not know it last year but she knows it now, someone has told her.'

'Die for Louis Duville? How childish! Work and pleasure mean more to him than love. My child, you must tell Léopoldine to forget this business.'

'When one is loved one is afraid of death and when one isn't one longs for it. Keep this letter, colonel, and if anything should happen give it to Louis Duville. It will be safe with you; if I had it my family might find it and read it; I should also be afraid of mislaying it, for my life is uncertain,' she said, then she drank a glass of syrup and left.

The colonel shook his head: 'Childishness, childishness,' he muttered, and after throwing the letter into one of the drawers of his writing-table, he went on reading.

However, his conversation with the girl had disconcerted him. 'Most young people are ready to give their lives for an ideal. Something must be done,' he thought, and resolved to save Léopoldine from death, he set out for Valronce. Mme Duville was taking her annual cure, her husband was in the mountains and Louis Duville, who ran the business alone when his father was away, had just come in and was breathing the evening air outside the house. The abrupt manner with which the colonel stopped his car, got out of it and slammed the door, made Louis Duville think that he had come to announce an important military event: 'Well, then, this is a pretty state of affairs,' shouted the colonel, walking resolutely towards him. 'This is no time for joking, I assure you. Where is Léopoldine? Have you news of her?'

'I don't understand why you ask me that, uncle.'

'You don't understand, come now. Be serious, my friend. The situation is grave, she is probably desperate. A friend of Léopoldine has entrusted me with the last will and testament of this wretched girl whose head you have turned. You must be mad. Fifteen years old! Her will. Do you even know what that means? She loves you and wants to put an end to her life, if she hasn't already done so. You will confess that that is going a bit far.'

'My dear uncle, you greatly surprise me.'

'I surprise you? Is that all you can find to say? You are surprised? That is enough for you. Come now, there are other things in life for a man than women; there is love.'

'I have my commitments,' answered Louis Duville.

'Yes, pleasure and business; and while you spend your time at restaurants, casinos and galas, with whom? I might ask – and I don't want to hear the answer because I know it – poor Léopoldine is deciding between the rope, the river or the pistol.'

'What an exaggeration! I have only seen Léopoldine once, and that was nearly a year ago.'

'Only once? Once too often.'

'I could scarcely have done less.'

'Then you should have done more.'

'More?'

'Yes, because if she knew you better she would certainly love you less. She has made an ideal figure of you which can never be proved false until you condescend to give her a chance of comparing it with the sad reality. You could have made that sacrifice.'

'All this is embarrassing, unpleasant, grotesque. Has Léopoldine then nothing better to do than die of love?'

'What do you expect, young people are easily carried away and at Léopoldine's age one kills oneself over a silly trifle. You have the proof. I tell you again, she has made her will. Think it

over, and don't let negligence make you a murderer. I am going to Luchon tomorrow. I trust I shall not receive bad news there.'

At dusk that day, Louis Duville stopped his car in the country and walked through woods as far as Léopoldine's house. It was a small château with four turrets, completely covered by virgin vine which made it a vegetable monument, set quivering by the slightest breath of wind. A lighted lamp on a balcony kept the bats away from a room from which came the strains of distant music, unlike any he had heard. On the doorstep were two baskets of mushrooms. Louis Duville knocked on the door for some time; a maidservant opened it, stared at him, and shut it in his face without asking his business. Disconcerted, stunned by surprise, he looked up and saw Léopoldine on the lighted balcony. 'I am coming,' she called, and came down from her window.

'Did you lose your way in the woods?' she said.

'The scenery and the lanes change with the seasons. Sometimes the countryside is transformed from one hour to another, and in order not to get lost one has to know it well, and know it well at different times. Where were you going? Or, rather, where were you meaning to go?'

'I was coming to see you.'

'Why do you lie?'

'I am not lying. I think of you often and miss you, wishing I were not as I am. My life makes me very unhappy.'

'In my case it is my youth that makes me very unhappy.'

The lamp burned on the balcony and the bats flew past each other in the liquid night air. It was almost cold. 'Come,' said Léopoldine, and they went to sit on a fallen tree.

* * *

The birth of an era cannot be foreseen. On one side of the same existence there was Louis Duville and Mme Zaraguirre, Paris, dresses, jewels, endless nights, the bondage of being the lover of an irreproachable woman whom desertion would destroy, and on the other side there was Louis Duville and Léopoldine, the black ribbon round her neck, the country, meetings at cross-roads and the silences of love.

Over three years passed thus, in which apparently nothing was changed in anybody's life.

M. Duville and his son went together to their work; Saturdays brought Louis Duville to Paris; he spent his holidays in big hotels with Mme Zaraguirre, the Dajeus and their friends; M. Duville collected plants; Mme Duville took her cure; the colonel wrote his memoirs; each October brought M. Zaraguirre back to Valronce and then Louis Duville found excuses to be absent.

At the time of her first conversation with M. Zaraguirre, Léopoldine did not know the reasons for his separation from his wife, and although she had since been told them she had continued to feign ignorance, out of tact and affection for him. She still confided in him. 'In matters that are most important to us, we must keep our jealousy patient,' he told her one day. 'Love dies because we secretly believe it to be an illusion.'

'I have no need to be jealous and I have no illusions. I shall marry Louis, you will see To worry him I sometimes tell him that I am making up my mind between you both. I tell him that I love you as much as him.'

'By "as much as" you mean "in a different way."'

'Different ways can be equally valuable. They can even be rivals.'

'Yes, but nobody likes being loved "in a different way", even if it means that they are loved more.'

'Then it is him that I love in a different way,' she said; and she asked him if he would come to her wedding.

'Yes, I shall travel from Tijo especially for it.'

The extravagances of love are pleasant and reassuring; they defy analysis and escape criticism. At Valronce all the neighbours took an interest in Léopoldine's love affair. M. and Mme Duville supported it and at every visit M. Zaraguirre encouraged a feeling whose triumph would bring about his wife's undoing. This idea pleased him, and while he smiled on the future Louis Duville vainly tried to free himself from Mme Zaraguirre: 'There can be nothing worse than to love a man one does not trust,' she told him. 'If you were unfaithful to me I should kill myself.' She also said: 'You work too hard, darling, you are tired and that keeps us apart. Let's go and rest in the country and I will pamper you,' and finally she announced one evening that she was going to get a divorce: 'I have had enough of living as we do and have been to see the Dajeus' lawyer.'

'A divorce? Why?'

'Because I hate false positions. If I were free, we should both be free.'

'No more than at present. You have to answer to no one.'

'No, but at present it is not a life. I want a real life for us both, in a real home. It seems to me that we have a right to it.'

At these words Louis Duville pretended to have forgotten a business appointment, and left abruptly.

On the following day Léopoldine celebrated her seventeenth birthday. For this occasion she had organised a picnic in the woods: 'My picnic will be no ordinary party,' she told Louis Duville. 'My father will be there as a Turk, in a turban, my mother as herself, the colonel as a colonel, and your parents. My best friends are coming, there will be seventeen of us and you will sit next to me. I have asked them at dusk because it was dusk when you came to see me for the first time. Time goes fast when one is in love. Three years! Just think!'

'You are not only in my heart, but in my soul as well,' he had answered.

'And what will you give me for my birthday?'

'A thought.'

'Oh! That is too much.'

Proud of being loved by a man of his age, she played at dominating him and had insisted on his helping her to

receive her guests. Nothing could have given Louis Duville greater pleasure than to obey her, and at seven o'clock he was beneath her window. She appeared on her balcony, a black ribbon round her neck, wearing an old-fashioned, dark, daring dress that enhanced the brightness of her youth: 'Wait,' she said, and a moment later she was in his arms. The guests arrived together, bringing flowers and presents. They jostled each other, embraced and laughed. Léopoldine's father, dressed as a Turk, jumped about beside her and her mother never stopped saying: 'Seventeen, seventeen, Heavens, how the children are growing up; who would have thought it?

Pyramids of roses bordered the path which led through the woods to the house, by the side of a lake, where the picnic was prepared. Léopoldine walked alone in front of her guests; they followed her in a procession and she led them to their places. Unless a thunderstorm breaks out, no wind blows on the last days of July in continental countries. Carps broke the mirror of light that the moon spread on the lake; it was warm; pink, blue and mauve plates, set on the leaves of chestnut-trees, resembled large pressed flowers. There were chicken dishes, salad and fruit, and jugs of wine surrounded the birthday cake whose seventeen candles illuminated the meal. Every creation contains a prophecy and artists, by telling us truths that they have not foreseen, fill us either with fear or with longing for the world to which we return.

Léopoldine's picnic was in league with eternity. It fell from the sky, grace descended on it and each of the guests suddenly had the feeling of being a blessed shadow on the earth. Léopoldine's father got a little drunk and during the dessert he shouted: 'Musicians, where are you?' Young men and girls rose and Léopoldine, whose shoulder brushed against Louis Duville's, rose with them. They took up their guitars and violins and she sang a song she had composed:

> *Tous les pirates du Levant*
> *N'ont d'autre idole*
> *Qu'une boussole*
> *Tous les pirates du Levant*
> *Ont des captives au couvent.*
>
> *Une pauvre enfant de l'école*
> *S'en va rêvant*
> *Au jour levant*
> *Une pauvre enfant de l'école*
> *Cherche le vent qui la cajole*
>
> *Et elle brode un paravent*
> *Où l'oiseau vole*
> *Mais ne s'envole*
> *Et elle brode un paravent*
> *Pour un pirate du Levant.*
>
> *Quand elle pense aux métropoles*
> *Un mot souvent*
> *Rit dans le vent*
> *Quand elle pense aux métropoles*
> *Tout en brodant son âme folle*

> *Pour un pirate du Levant*
> *Qui est frivole*
> *Et sans parole*
> *Pour un pirate du Levant*
> *Une enfant brode un paravent.*

After exclamations and applause, Léopoldine yielded to their entreaties and began her song again.

'A pirate from the Levant? How does she think of such things?' said her mother.

'Yes, a pirate from the Levant, what is that exactly?' asked Mme Duville.

'What one can't understand is usually inexplicable,' answered her husband.

'I shall not blow out the candles on my birthday cake,' Léopoldine declared. 'When the candles are out, the party is over.'

She removed the candles, put them in candlesticks, cut the cake, offered it to everyone and served Louis Duville the last. 'Open your hand. Here is a thought,' he said, and in her outstretched palm he placed a sapphire thought which she clasped in her hand all night long.

* * *

Two days later Mme Zaraguirre received a letter from Louis Duville. She had just come in and was sitting at her dressing-table with Mme Dajeu: 'I am so tired I can't see, I'm going to bed,' she said.

'I envy you. I have got to get dressed and go out to dinner, and what a dinner . . .!'

'I look terrible,' remarked Mme Zaraguirre.

'Men are lucky; even when they are dead it doesn't show. Nothing alters them,' said Mme Dajeu.

It was then that her lady's maid brought Mme Zaraguirre the evening paper and a letter.

'Why, it's a letter from Louis. I'm sure he is writing to ask me to forgive him.'

'Forgive him?'

'Yes, last time he came to see me he left me all of a sudden, without a word, without even kissing me, but I don't mind: poor thing, he is almost as tired as I am.

She took the letter from its envelope, unfolded it, placed it on her dressing-table, glanced at the opening lines and burst out laughing: 'Ah, I was right, listen to this: "Darling, be indulgent and forgive me for leaving so soon the other day. I know what I am feeling but not what I am doing; I am working too hard, I don't sleep enough and I am less and less master of my own time. Under these conditions, how can you expect me to be myself and how can I be happy when circumstances prevent me from thinking only of your happiness? Your happiness! My darling, I want you to be happy, you must be, it is my desire and my torment . . ."'

Mme Zaraguirre held a comb in her left hand and as she read she passed it through her hair with a circular motion.

'What a man, what devotion!' said Mme Dajeu.

'He is killing himself,' answered Mme Zaraguirre and she went on reading out loud: '"And I am going to disappoint you once more: it is impossible for me to come to Paris next Saturday. Some colleagues from abroad are coming to Valronce and I must be there. You see that I am not deserting you for my own pleasure.

'"What can I tell you to interest you? It is very hot, everything is scorched; one burns until five o'clock, it's unbearable, but luckily the nights are cool and we dine out of doors nearly every evening. Yesterday, can you believe it, I even went to a picnic near Dentelle (Dentelle, what memories!) beside a lake with some rather mad people whose sons were childhood friends of mine. Neither of them was there, which disappointed me. It was the seventeenth birthday of their sister, Léopoldine. You would like her very much."'

'He thinks only of you,' Mme Dajeu put in.

'"She dances, writes poetry and composes songs that she sings marvellously. And with all that she is simplicity itself; she is simple in the way that some absent-minded people are. I don't know how many times I thought of you as I watched her. It is owing to you that I can now appreciate such naïve people and occasions, which in the old days I used to avoid. You have taught me everything. Were it not for you and the years that we have spent together, I should have been bored at this provincial dinner-party and should have gone back to Valronce furious at having wasted my time. The weather was superb, as it happened. It was like Austria in the summer: the lake, music, a blue night sky, white wine, do you remember? It wrings my heart."'

'He brings everything back to you,' Mme Dajeu interposed.

'Ah! don't interrupt me, please,' exclaimed Mme Zaraguirre, and she went on: '"Yesterday, a star piloted the invisible vessel of the moon, whose sail was nearly round, and while everything around us was quivering and we heard the whispering of wild life on a night in July, I thought of you, imprisoned in the walls of Paris. The most innocent pleasures sometimes give us a bad conscience. Yes, I thought of you and felt that my pleasure at being there was guilty. It is not other eyes, other arms, other hair that a woman need fear, but the traces of mystery in nature, the power of silence and meditations that brave great distances. You are in no danger of being forgotten, I assure you. And speaking of forgetting, I must not forget to tell you that Léopoldine's parents may be sending her to Paris this autumn to finish her musical studies. She will be lost there. I have promised to look after her and you must help me. I am delighted for your sake, she will amuse and interest you, I am sure.

'"Darling, even if I knew how to write, this letter would still represent the monotony of my life. I am afraid of boring you and, what it worse, that is not my only fear: I am afraid of being detained here longer than usual this year and would be easier in my mind if I knew that you were out of Paris in this heat. Don't change the date we decided on for going to the South. Go with the Dajeus and I shall join you there. Don't be angry with me, I beg you. I am miserable about it, you can be sure of that. What have I heard lately that is worth repeating? Oh! yes, yesterday, at the end of the evening, Léopoldine's father who was dressed as a Turk said to me: 'My sons see everything pink and my daughter everything blue. That will always keep them apart.' Wasn't that rather funny? And what was even better is that Léopoldine put her hand over his mouth and whispered: 'Take care, the countryside is full of fairies, don't tell them our secrets.' That gives you an idea of what the family is like. What a pity that you weren't there. You would have enjoyed it. Léopoldine and you are made for each other.'"

Suddenly, Mme Zaraguirre fell silent. She took the letter, crumpled it up, threw it on the ground, rose and stamped on it: 'Ah! A whole love-letter to tell me that I am no longer loved,' she cried.

'Darling, you are mad! You have lost your head,' replied Mme Dajeu.

'No, I am not mad. My husband always said that love fills the imagination before taking possession of the heart.'

'Your husband? This has nothing to do with him. What has he got to do with it?'

'Louis cannot hide it. His imagination has been stolen away. Ah! It's abominable! Ah! I have ceased to exist; and to think that I have wasted so many years, yes, so many years with that ungrateful man!'

'You have wasted nothing at all, you are more beautiful than ever and you are going to bed. You are so tired that you see things all wrong and tomorrow you will laugh at your fears. Louis speaks only of you in his letter.'

Mme Zaraguirre wept. 'You will get drunk on tears,' Mme Dajeu went on, 'Louis adores you and when you see him you will read in his eyes ...'

'That he doesn't love me any more, no, no ...'

'Darling, he has been at your feet for four years, he lives only for you, you have no reasons to mistrust him. Is that true or not? No woman could have a more attentive lover, don't be ungrateful.'

Mme Dajeu picked up the letter, smoothed it, put it back in its envelope and slipped it under one of the candlesticks on the dressing-table.

'Love fills the imagination before taking possession of the heart,' Mme Zaraguirre repeated, sobbing.

'A moment ago you were mad and now you are stupid. Do you even know what imagination is? Well, it is precisely the opposite of reality. And you torture yourself for that? No, no, I forbid it. "Love fills the imagination before taking possession etc.", an artistic thought! It means nothing. Calm yourself and do stop always going back to your husband.'

'Going back to my husband?'

'Yes, I'm not joking. As a result of talking about him, sometimes to make Louis Duville jealous and sometimes to amuse yourself by the sighs of your women friends, you have ended by taking him seriously. It is absurd. Come, I am going to help you to bed.'

Mme Zaraguirre was no longer crying: 'No, you are in a hurry, you are dining out, you have to get dressed. Go away, leave me, I beg you.'

'You will be sensible?'

'I shall be sensible.'

'Well, then, good night darling, good night, I am miserable at seeing you like this; what else can I do for you?'

'You could have scolded me, but it is too late. Go off, hurry, you haven't a minute to lose.'

On her way out Mme Dajeu rang for the maid without telling Mme Zaraguirre, who was already going over Louis Duville's letter: "'It was the seventeenth birthday . . . I don't know how many times I thought of you as I watched her . . . She is simple in the way that some absent-minded people are . . . She will amuse and interest you . . . You are made for each other." And I am a burden, deceived, ridiculous,' she murmured.

She felt a presence in the room and turned: it was her lady's maid.

'You are here,' she said.

'Madame rang?'

'I may have. Pack my new dresses and bring me a travelling suit. Mme Dajeu is expecting me at her house. We have decided to leave tonight for the South.'

One hour later, a taxi drove her with her luggage to a hotel where she spent the night.

* * *

Mme Zaraguirre arrived in South America at the time when her husband left for his annual visit to Europe. She took a car

and went to Tijo. Her mind was filled by a vision of the places and people who continued to live and to flourish in spite of her absence; her thoughts were those of a dead woman and she did not see the countryside through the windows as she travelled. She heard dance bands, the bells on sleighs in the Tyrol, the clink of ice in glasses, Mme Dajeu's voice, and it seemed to her that the car was gliding on carpets through the shops, restaurants and drawing-rooms of Paris.

It was evening. A servant whom she did not know opened the door at Tijo. 'M. Zaraguirre. Go and fetch him,' she said. And when he stood back to let her pass she shook her head, stayed outside and looked into the house through a window. M. Zaraguirre was entertaining some friends. On seeing him cross the drawing-room to go out she ran away into the garden and leant against a tree. M. Zaraguirre stopped on the threshold: 'Who is there?' he asked. He came forward into the twilight, repeated: 'Who is there?' then distinguishing a pale figure, he approached it. 'You,' murmured Mme Zaraguirre, and with a bewildered start she threw herself on his breast. He did not push her away but he did not embrace her and allowed her to weep. After a moment, he tried to lift up her face.

'No, no,' she said, pressing closer to him.

'Well,' answered M. Zaraguirre, 'cry, cry on my shoulder if you only came back for that.'